Martina Warren

Against the World

AF204992

Martina Warren

Against the World

:Halfies, demons, angels

JustFiction Edition

Impressum/Imprint (nur für Deutschland/only for Germany)
Bibliografische Information der Deutschen Nationalbibliothek: Die Deutsche Nationalbibliothek verzeichnet diese Publikation in der Deutschen Nationalbibliografie; detaillierte bibliografische Daten sind im Internet über http://dnb.d-nb.de abrufbar.
Alle in diesem Buch genannten Marken und Produktnamen unterliegen warenzeichen-, marken- oder patentrechtlichem Schutz bzw. sind Warenzeichen oder eingetragene Warenzeichen der jeweiligen Inhaber. Die Wiedergabe von Marken, Produktnamen, Gebrauchsnamen, Handelsnamen, Warenbezeichnungen u.s.w. in diesem Werk berechtigt auch ohne besondere Kennzeichnung nicht zu der Annahme, dass solche Namen im Sinne der Warenzeichen- und Markenschutzgesetzgebung als frei zu betrachten wären und daher von jedermann benutzt werden dürften.

Coverbild: www.ingimage.com

Verlag: JustFiction! Edition ist ein Imprint der
LAP LAMBERT Academic Publishing GmbH & Co. KG
Heinrich-Böcking-Str. 6-8, 66121 Saarbrücken, Deutschland
Telefon +49 681 37 20 310, Telefax +49 681 37 20 310-9
Email: info@justfiction-edition.com

Herstellung in Deutschland:
Schaltungsdienst Lange o.H.G., Berlin
Books on Demand GmbH, Norderstedt
Reha GmbH, Saarbrücken
Amazon Distribution GmbH, Leipzig
ISBN: 978-3-8454-4511-3

Imprint (only for USA, GB)
Bibliographic information published by the Deutsche Nationalbibliothek: The Deutsche Nationalbibliothek lists this publication in the Deutsche Nationalbibliografie; detailed bibliographic data are available in the Internet at http://dnb.d-nb.de.
Any brand names and product names mentioned in this book are subject to trademark, brand or patent protection and are trademarks or registered trademarks of their respective holders. The use of brand names, product names, common names, trade names, product descriptions etc. even without a particular marking in this works is in no way to be construed to mean that such names may be regarded as unrestricted in respect of trademark and brand protection legislation and could thus be used by anyone.

Cover image: www.ingimage.com

Publisher: JustFiction! Edition
is an imprint of the publishing house
LAP LAMBERT Academic Publishing GmbH & Co. KG
Heinrich-Böcking-Str. 6-8, 66121 Saarbrücken, Germany
Phone +49 681 37 20 310, Fax +49 681 37 20 310-9
Email: info@justfiction-edition.com

Printed in the U.S.A.
Printed in the U.K. by (see last page)
ISBN: 978-3-8454-4511-3

"Against the World"

"Against the World"

By: Martina Warren

This book is dedicated to my friends, family, high school teachers and my boyfriend for supporting me. Thank you all for being there.

"Against the World"

Prologue: Anger

What was this feeling that she felt? It isn't any other happy or sad emotion that she could easily identify, she knew this much. She placed her hand on her forehead, rubbing it out of frustration. She's not upset. She's not even sad...

The glass plate flew over her head smashing against the wall behind her with a loud crash. She closed her eyes, her blood went cold and fear crept in her body. "Get out! G.E.T. O.U.T!" Her body trembled over the coldness of the thrower 's voice. She couldn't understand those two words that her step mother had said to her with such hatred. "What did I tell you, freak! Get out!" her words were drowned with another crash of a plate she had thrown after her sixth word. "Why? Why? I trusted you!" the girl screeched out and another crash the third plate hit her in the middle of her forehead, knocking her off balance and in a fit of darkness. She trusted her...And she betrayed her. She had been rejected...because of her curse or gift she had been rejected. Her blood covered the marble floor as it flowed down the girl's forehead.

Yes this pain in her heart was caused by her step-mother...The woman that her caring real father had married two years ago. The woman that she could related the most with had caused her such physical and mentally pain.

"Esmee, please don't make any mistakes. It isn't your fault that she's filing for a divorce." Her father told her 20 minutes ago. He looked like a mess, his appearance had change in really short time. The words that he spoke was mere lies. The truth

9

behind those words, 'It's all your fault, but I can't tell you that.'. He shifted in his

chair, before standing up uncomfortable. "I hope you get well soon, love." He spoke

dully, without any feelings behind his words and Esmee flinched in the hospital bed.

He walked towards the door opening with such a desperate force, wanting to leave

the room from the person who ruined his life in a mere day. "Dad..." The words left

Esmee's lips without thinking, "Please stay, I'm sorry.." but her father didn't even

hesitate. He ignored his daughter plead, and left the room, closing the door behind

him.

She was angry, this anger wasn't for her ex-step mother or her father. This anger is directed to herself for even telling her step-mother her secret. A secret that the Christian Church viewed disapproval of. She could see the dead just barely. She saw shadows gliding down the hospital halls...Crying and screaming, one of them was angry because his family left him here to die. These shadows had scared her. A tear slid down her eye, and now she knew...She now knew that she was scared of rejection.

There was a soft knock on the door, it opened moments later revealing the hospital nurse. She smiled nicely at Esmee, with such kindness that she didn't know a human could have...it's hard to believe that this kindness could be easily replaced by hatred of her secret.

She held a purple plastic vase filled with a few lilies. Her favorite color and flower.

"Esmee, dear. Look at what someone brought you." She kindly said, walking through the room toward the window. She opened the curtains gently and the sunlight came through the window in a second. "I'll just set this here." She placed the vase on the window ceil, in the front lines of sunlight.

"Here's the card that came with it."

The nurse handed Esmee, a small white card.

'Please get well soon, everyone over here misses you!-Aly'
"Thank you."

The nurse nodded her head, "Your welcome sweetie. If you need anything please press the button by your bedside." and she to left.

Tears rolled down her blue eyes, she was indeed scared of rejection. Thank the heaven's that she had at least one friend in the world. Now this feeling have increased. She was angry. She was angry of herself and now the world.

.~.

"So you gave it to her, Nurse?" a man in his early 20's asked the nurse that just walked out of Esmee's room. The nurse shut the door close before she spoke kindly to the man beside her.

"Yes, I did sir and she loved it. Why didn't you write your own name on the card?" The nurse
asked, out of curiosity, and the 22 year old man, just shook his shoulders "Because I just don't want her to know that it was from me. It would have risked my career." The man replied hotly, before leaving the woman behind confused.

Chapter One: A Deeper Sense

Esmee sat up from her hospital bed with a tired yawn avoiding looking at the four white walls that are void of any other colors. "Your leaving today, right, Esmee?" Aly asked with a calm voice, sitting in the corner chair beside the bed. Esmee nodded her head sadly, "Yeah if today's Thursday. I don't have enough money to stay another night." She touched her bandaged forehead, and winced at the small amount of pain shot through her body.

Aly shook her head disappointing look over her figure. "It can't be that bad, Esmee." Aly replied with a carefree attitude. Esmee always liked to be overdramatic over small stuff so this would be normal for her friend. Esmee stared blankly at Aly, "My step-mother threw a glass plate against my forehead and I was left bleeding on the floor for 30 minutes straight. So you tell me if it isn't that bad." There wasn't any emotion in her voice, when she spoke this. She hid it well. She hid the anger she felt behind an empty void of worthless feelings in the back of her mind.

Aly could not fully understand Esmee's explanation, "Esmee, this is getting old. Is it time for you to tell the truth?"

Something came across of Esmee's face, it was a mix of both hurt and pain, then with anger again. Her friend did not believe her. She even denied the flowers that she send yesterday afternoon. She crunched her hands into a pair of fist and her teeth clinched together.

She was ready to say the two words that her step-mother had said to her the other night before sending her to this place. Her blood chilled and she could feel it became thicker.

She was slowly suffocating...

"Get out. Get the hell of this room!" Her voice was cold and angry. The emotions could be seen from her blue wild eyes that are blazing flames. No one believed what happened. Aly is rejecting her. She doesn't need her or anyone else for the matter.

Aly looked at Esmee in shock as she stood up from her chair. Esmee's body slowly trembled in anger and somewhat fear.

She doesn't want to be anyone's friend if she has to face rejection anyway.
"Esmee, are you all right?" her friend voice was filled with concern, and Esmee eyes hardened at the thought of it all being fake.

She was a fake.
She made her way toward Esmee, but Esmee took a swipe at her face. Aly barely dodged the strike.

What's wrong with Esmee? Aly was confused, at this sudden outburst and then she felt hurt. Esmee was willing to attack her without even pausing.

"Stay away from me! If you don't believe me when I tell you the truth, why should I need you in my life?"

There was a minute of an awkward silence.
"You don't really mean this do you?"

"I don't need friends that don't trust me." snarled Esmee, and she knew later she would definitely regret this choice of words and action.

Suddenly a Nurse opened the door of the room with worry, "What's all the noise about?"

Esmee turned away, the room turned cold and colder by the minute.

"Please get her out of the room," She almost pleaded.

The Nurse placed her hand on Aly's shoulder.

"Your upsetting the patient, please leave the room." The nurse said, and Aly found herself nodded her head. What had come over Esmee to do such a thing to her?

When the two people exited the room, closing the door behind them, Esmee felt another person or spirit within the same room. How she feel this? The room is getting colder and colder, and she could see her breathe right in front of her.

"Bravo, bravo. You managed to drive away your only friend." Said a cheery voice, softly clapping his hands. Esmee turned to the window sharply, suddenly remembering that she was still in her hospital night gown and her hair is unbrushed.

The window was open, and sitting on the ledge was a boy. A boy her age, and he doesn't seemed human at all. He's cat like, "It's none of your concern, get out of my room." Esmee replied coldly, and the boy didn't look affected by her words or tone unlike Aly.

He climbed into the window with grace, and smile brightly at Esmee, who found this boy a freak and he was very strange.

"Actually it's not really your room, it's the hospital's, matter of fact it's really isn't the hospital's room it's the government's." came the smartass comment from the teen. The sun shined on him, making him seem very bright.. almost like he was placing a spell on her.

"Whatever." muttered Esmee, wishing, no hoping that the nurse would come back in the room and escort this person out.

He seemed to read her mind and he frowned.

"She won't come back you know." His voice suddenly turned dark, and Esmee looked at him with an appealing new look.

He chuckled darkly, "Oh I'm sorry, I forgot to introduce myself. I'm Trace Wolf, a new student at James Wood High."

Something within her sparked. A deeper sense of hate and sadness planted itself within the darkest place of her mind.

"I'm Esmee Lock, 12th year in James Wood High." She uttered a reply, before almost gliding toward her bed finding it suddenly attractive for some obvious reason.

Trace looked over his shoulder for a moment before glancing back to Esmee with a look that she clearly couldn't read.

"It's a pleasure to meet you, now my time has ended and I must take my leave. See you at school." He waved off going back to the window ledge- "There is a door here you know"

His cheerful attitude seemed to come back when he reached the ledge,

"I know, but it's a lot more fun climbing down." and with that he actually lurched himself out of the window, scaring Esmee. What idiot would jump out of a second story window anyway? Esmee looked out the window and down to the ground, as panic stuck on her face.

"Trace!" She called, she didn't see any motionless flat body below or anyone that looked like Trace. It's like he completely disappeared in thin air which was completely impossible.

Somewhere in the Demon Realm

"I found her Kaden, that half mortal girl." Trace exclaimed, a darker hair male grinned at the news that his partner Trace had given.

"Perfect." Kaden smirked, before turning to the corner of the room which was drowned with human blood.

"Isn't it perfect, Cain Heartwell? This girl that you had been refusing to give us her whereabouts will help us find her dear demon mother, "Kaden almost mocked the lowly human in the corner who was bleeding heavily from the cuts and slashes they had thrashed upon him.

He did not know what they were talking about. What girl? He didn't hide anyone from them. Pain came through his body and Kaden caught this. He walked over to Cain and grasped his chin, picking it up to his eye level. Cain stared into the hatred of his blackish red eyes. There was no mercy in them.

"I'll let you see her suffer before killing you off, Heartwell. I'm feeling that generous." He said, roughly letting go of his chin before Cain could have any chance to do anything. His breath went hollow and Kaden laughed.

"Humans, weak and useless" He mocked, kicking Cain on his side. Cain let out a hurtful scream. Trace walked beside his boss, and looked at his adoptive cousin with a deep hate.

"Want me to go get her now? She's just in one of those human hospitals." Trace mocked the word human hospitals. Kaden nodded his head in agreement. This was a good time to get the information of this demon wrench mother of the half mortal.

Trace, getting the message, twisted his waist a bit and then out of the particles of pollution in the thick air of the room, appeared an old style door. He twisted the knob, the door flew opened on contact.

"This won't be long," Trace said confidently, walking through the portal. When the last piece of his body was through the door, it disappeared slowly.

Kaden walked to the next room in the lair, figuring that Cain was definitely too weak to move. He shouldn't be too much of a problem.

The chains that held Cain in place to the wall is very tight, giving him almost no room to move about. Hopelessness started to fill his mind, but he shook it off without any hesitation. He have to get out. He had to stop Trace.

He pulled his right arm and the chain clanked at the pull. He needed to be quick. His left arm was close to the pocket that held his pistol...If he could reach it there was hope.
He then moved his hips to his left side of the chain and suddenly he touched his coat pocket.

The pistol felt heavy on his three bruised figures. He almost didn't have enough strength to pull the human weapon out.

His joints began to hurt...His skin was sore, and sure enough he has at least one black eye. A few of his ribs were broken; he heard them crack hours ago with the intensive pain. The cuts and slashes were all over his legs and arms. They really did a number

17

on him when he refused to help them with their plan. Could he really make it out? Him a lowly human that could die easily?

He aimed the pistol to the chain that held him, 'Come on pull the trigger,' He chanted in his head, until he surprisingly pulled the trigger,

The noise echoed throughout the room and Cain knew he had a very short time before Kaden came back in and checked it out. The chains came loose and Cain pulled down, making it come off its hinges. He bent over, getting the feel back to his body, and almost screamed as the intense pain crept into his body once more from the wounds he had.

He could hear the sound of footsteps radiate from the walls of the room. Kaden was coming…

Cain limped to the spot that Trace disappeared out of- "From the heavens I need to leave." He chanted out loud, and suddenly a golden door appeared in front of him, a portal.

"Come back here, Heartwell!" Kaden's voice radiated angry, the whole room began to shake violently. The hair on Cain's neck rose, and he limped towards the golden door desperately. Kaden was quick, very quick. "I should have broken your arms and legs." He growled clawing Cain's back in a rage, Cain turned the doorknob and then his vision turned red. He felt the skin on his back begin to open with the impact of Kaden's inhuman claws.

"N-No" muttered Cain, he felt his whole body went limp, a wave of dizziness slammed into Cain's head. His vision getting blurry, damn his weakness. Damn his human body. Kaden pulled back his claws for a second strike. Cain turned the knob once more, the door opened, and a bright, shining light through the entrance.

He could feel Kaden back off, covering his eyes from the light. Cain limped through the doorway and when the door closed behind him, he fell to his knees. His breathing became hollow again, as he crawled through the halls of the realms trying to get up many times, falling back down. Cain only had two near death experiences before. This is one of them.

"I should have listened to father about the book of Eli and stayed out of trouble." Cain hoarsely told himself, before he got back his motivation to keep on walking, or crawling, to his location. He could taste his own blood within his thin chapped lips, before he coughed it out. The taste was bitter and the scent disgusted him. How much blood had he lost? His human body was made of eight pints of blood, and a human could barely live on four pints with a blood donation in a short time. He needed serious help.

His body finally gave out when he arrived at the last realm of the hall. It was the human realm, his home.

Trace...The girl...Mortal...Save
These words kept on repeating in his head.

Light footsteps that was what he now heard through his ears. He looked up weakly, and knowing it wasn't Kaden or Trace. They weren't that light on their feet. What met him almost surprised him. It was a girl with long flowing blond hair wearing a white dress. She has a pair of wings on her back, white. She must be an angel.

"Your poor thing..." and then rest he blacked out

Chapter Two: Let the Snow Fall

March 28, 1990

There were small snowflakes falling from the clouds above and onto the hard and dirty ground. Kaden watched in amazement. He loved the snow and he loved how cold the snow felt. He almost danced around in it if his mother wasn't with him smiling, cheerfully at her son's behavior.

One more snowflake fell onto Kaden's head and he shook it off within a few seconds. "I want to build a snowman, but there isn't much snow to do it. I want to do a snow angel but I still have the same problem." Kaden stated to his watching mother.

"I'm sure, it will snow all night and then you will be able to do those things, honey." Hope Slade, Kaden's mother, spoke softly. Kaden nodded his head in agreement, just as a huge sloppily made snowball flew through the air and hit the back of Kaden's head. Kaden flinched at the cold impact.

"Look what we have here, boys. Kaden brought his little sick mother to the park to play. Isn't that sad?" mocked a boy a few years older than Kaden. Kaden eyes automatically went downward toward the ground, as the boys came closer.

"I suggest you boys to leave and go home," demanded Hope, with authority in her tone. The three bullies just blinked at her and then began to laugh aloud and Hope could feel her blood boiling. These kids had no manners at all! "And you'll do what lady? Your weak and helpless, all women are like that anyway," The bully at the front snarled, and grabbed Hope's hand and jerked her forward just to prove a point. Hope

20

gasped at the sudden action.

"Let go of me, you bastard!" She screeched at the child, who had the courage to even touch an adult. The child she screeched at wasn't actually a child. He was about 15 years of age. She tried to jerk her hand out of his hold, but couldn't. Her body was weak and worn out from her recent sickness. She really doesn't have the strength to fight.

His grip tightened, "A second ago I would have, but with your mouth now I won't" then he grinned widely, "Boys, let show this witch a proper lesso-"

Kaden fist connected to the bully's nose wildly. He let go of Hope's hand and held his own hand over his nose in pain.

"You little bra-" Kaden fist connected once more, and the bully fell backward on the snowy path. Kaden eyes was wild shade of red,
"Touch her again, and you're dead." Kaden snarled, at the fallen bully. Then he noticed his two followers stepping forward, Kaden glared at them with a killing look. They easy backed off after that.

The Kaden that Hope knew was no more in front of her eyes. Her Kaden wouldn't hurt a fly much less punch or beat up people.

Hope actually felt fear bobbing up in her nervous system. 'Kaden, stop' his mother wanted to say, but she found out that she couldn't speak a thing.

The three bullies scrambled to their feet and fled the park, away from Kaden's murderous glare. Hope rubbed her hand softly over the bruise. Kaden back was turned from her and it's like he was battling an inner emotional battle over his own mind.

21

"Are you alright Mom?" He asked, his voice is deeper than his normal one a few minutes ago.

"Yes sweetie, thank you. Let's go home. this was enough fun for one day." Hope faked a smile as she stood and grabbed ahold of Kaden's hand. His hand tensed and then became relaxed the next second. He didn't glance at Hope at all.

"That's good, the sooner the better." Kaden stated, taking the lead walking Hope out of the snowy park and just by the street. He looked both ways, and then began to walk. His mother was a foot behind him, linked to his right hand.

They heard swerving and horns being blown and out of the cover of the falling snow appeared a white car, going over the speed limit obviously. Hope eyes widened, she knew it wasn't going to stop and Kaden figured this out too...and he let go of her hand and with a push Hope had fallen backward hard hitting her head on the snowy ground away from the street that the car had suddenly appeared like magic.

Horns began to blow once again and Hope raised her head out of the snow weakly, "Kaden!" She screamed, just as the car made an impact to Kaden's body. He flew high in the air, his eyes shut closed and blood flowed down his forehead.

He landed a few feet away from Hope. His blood soaked the snow under him and his eyes fluttered open weakly. Hope stared in horror, crawling towards her son. "K-Kaden, honey" She fell over his body, her head rested on her son's chest, as tears flow down her brown eyes. His blood stuck onto her side of her cheek.

"Mom?," He muttered weakly. Hope looked down at her dying son's grief stricken face. She couldn't do anything; no one was out and about. No one could get an ambulance here in time. He was losing so much blood and like every mother's nightmare. Her baby was slowly dying in her arms. "Yes, honey, mommy is here. Mommy is here." She sobbed through her tears pressing her ear on his chest where his heart was. His heart was slowing down and it missed a few beats. "It hurts...I don't want to die...It hurts so bad." He muttered painfully, "I know baby, I know. It's will all end soon."

There was a moment of silence. Neither of them spoke at all, each listening to the rhythm of each other's hearts, afraid to move from their place.

"I-I'm glad that you're alright mom."

His eyes slowly closed, a small smile reached his pale lips and then his heartbeat ended. Hope screamed, she screamed in pain and hurt. She screamed at the world and for God taking her beloved son away like this.

Chapter Three: So Near, but yet so Faraway

The blue sky showed the reflections of the future events of what was going to come. She could hear the birds singing happily from one nests near a tree that she was walking passed in the park. A short way from her house and the town's hospital. It was indeed a nice day, and this almost made Esmee smiled to her self a little bit at this. It does felt better to get out of the hospital and get some fresh air at some point. A few couples walked passed Esmee, with a huge smile on their faces, holding hands and talking to each other with such warmth. Why couldn't she have a special someone in her heart? Is it a crime to her? 'Boys likes girls with no brain and big boobs.' Esmee snarled to herself harshly. She have a brain, she could think and she has indeed no boobs. That is silly, guys isn't that shallow right?

Lock, dear, please walk this way.

Esmee heard a magical voice in her head in singing tone. Esmee shifted her bag over her arm, which the staff at the hospital gave her to place her things in. This must be her imagination and on cue her stomach began to growl hungry. Yes this was her imagination working with her hunger making her hear things that weren't really there to start off with.

She kept on walking without glancing in the direction that the voice called for her.

'Lock, its important please come this way.'

Her soul tugged in her body a little making her stopped walking completely. What was that feeling she felt? What was this voice? Something tugged on her once again, pulling her toward somewhere. Somewhere she didn't really want to go.

Her feet walked and think for her, as she walk blindly through some green bushes. A few kids pointed her way- "Mommy, why is she allow over there?"

She didn't hear no more. Where was she going? Why was her body acting without her own permission.

A little more. Don't worry you wouldn't be hurt.

She let her eyes glazed at her surroundings around her. This side of the park was where no one actually went at all. The trees and bushes blocked the view from the outside world. The sky above is clear, and to picture this completely is that this side of the park looks like a clearing in a woods or forest. Something caught her eye...It was a wooden cross. A small old wooden cross, that was nailed to the ground by the said tree. Esmee, tried to adjust her eyes to see the same on the cross. Someone died here...

The name was a blur, fading from the cross. She could barely read it...'Kaden Slade'? The name ran through her mind, and her blood went cold. It felt like she should be afraid... Her feet came into contact with something concrete. A sudden wave of dizziness over came her body, and she almost trip over her feet. An urge of vomiting struck her hard, and she almost obey, if it wasn't for the voice in her head telling her to tried to get use to it. The concrete below her feet she was walking on, used to be a street.

Her skin went pale, and then she saw someone a person, human lied out on the ground. She can tell it's a man, and for some reason she felt that she should know this person, but no name entered her mind. Her heart took a leap, when she took another close look and her feet stopped just before this man's body.

"Mr. Heartwell?" She muttered surprised, she kneed down pressing her hand on the young man chest. A hurtful moan left his lips, and she quickly moved her hand away. *'Help him. He needs help.'*

She knew this man before her. He was her history teacher at the end of her 11th grade year of highschool. His skin was really bruised, purplish. One of his eyes was blacked, and alot of scratches and cuts filled his once built body.

She let her hand pranced over his once well tone chest looking for any injuries, but of course she couldn't find anything above his clothes, duh.

25

He was still breathing, that is indeed a good sign. Esmee could felt the relief filled her heart. She unbuttoned a few buttons on his thick coat softly and quietly.

There was almost a pool of blood underneath this man, but most of the wounds invisible to her eye seemed to be closed. Strange... His coat flung open when she undid the last button, revealing his undershirt and blue jeans. He moaned once again painfully when she tugged on her shirt. Her heart beated faster than normal, she need to see if there was any wounds on his chest and maybe she could somewhat stop the bleeding. A red blood stain can be seen visiable on the center of his white shirt.

Fear, crept into Esmee's body. What if Mr. Heartwell opened his eyes. What would he think of her when she removed his shirt? Even through its for his health benefit. "We need to bring him to the hospital." Esmee whispered to herself,

'Explain to them, how he got this way? What will you say? Well he got hit by a car? He fell down? Those excuses wouldn't work...Maybe the car one would, but that doesn't explained the scratches and cuts that looked like it was made by claws on his WHOLE body.'

That voice in her head was right.

"Jen?" this snapped Esmee back to reality. Heartwell also known by Cain by his first name, struggled under Esmee's hands. His mouth began to move, and his eyes tried to open up out of his dream world and back into reality.

Esmee frozen in her spot, she stood still.

"Jen?" He muttered, his eyes fluttered opened for a split second, glancing over her face. He didn't really did anything else. His muscles began to flinched at her touch. He

26

moaned one more, pulling back his head backwards, away from her. His eyes fluttered closed and he was once again locked back into a dream state.

Esmee, could feel her heart hammered against her chest, and she let out a huge breathe. That was indeed close.

She tugged on his shirt up letting her see the front side of his muscular stomach, giving her good view. He was beautiful, every inch, and she could feel her face heated up. His beautiful skin is almost ruined due by the bruises, scratches and one cut that is opened bleeding slowly down his stomach. She have to stop it the best of her small abilities in first aid. She removed her hands from his body, almost in disappointing. She reached her bag, and pulled out a long shirt that she worn yesterday, that her father gave her.

She have to make a bandage...How to cut this..She wasn't strong enough to tear the said fabric apart. 'Oh lord please.' She almost plead, as she tried with all of her might to split the said fabric apart. It wiped sightly, and she cursed to herself with great determination, till FINALLY she wiped it apart, after seven fail attempts.

With the longer piece of fabric, she cleaned his cut the best she could. It wasn't much, but with no running water or any medicine what is expected.

She tied the smaller piece of fabric around his back over his stomach of the cut tightly. He flinched, all he could ever do is flinched and muttered somethings that doesn't make any sense to her. He's hurt and she have a sudden natural urge to heal or fix him up the best she could.

Her ears became even more redder, she is so immature about the opposite of gender.

She tugged down his shirt, revealing his face that seemed so much in pain.

'I need to get him out of here, but how? Many people will see him in this state, and surely call the police...but he also needs medical treatment...' Esmee hopelessly panicked to herself.

She glanced down at the passed out young man that she somewhat knew.
He seemed so near, but yet so faraway.

When Trace Wolf took a short visit to Esmee's hospital room, he was pissed off. She wasn't here! Not anymore and the blasted nurse said she released herself earlier today. He slapped his forehead, "I know it's going to be too easy if she's here." Trace talked to himself heading towards the window where he earlier jumped out of.

Now how will he find her again? He looked out the window, and almost couldn't believe on how much time flies when he traveled by portal.

He will surely meet Esmee, at school, but till then he just have to tell Kaden to be patient which is hard to do when that demon has a HUGE temper problem, with claws to make it bite.

Chapter Four- Don't Leave Me

May 23rd, 2003

Her laughter echoed through out the walls of his parents apartment making his heart beats fast through his chest and he could felt his cheeks glow a bright shade of red. Her hand rested on the side of his right cheek, and he didn't push it away nor flinch. He somewhat liked this warm touch, that she could offer him at this time of day.

28

"Cain, my love. I love you very much." The words mixed in her angels like voice, and Cain found himself leaning forward. "I love you as much as a man loves a woman." Cain muttered in her hand. Her smile widened brightly, she pulled back her hand and Cain seemed to miss her warming touch the moment she pulled away. He looked up at her glowing face, wondering if he had said something wrong when her beautiful laughter ended.

She leaned back on the coach and he did the same. "Then if you love me as much as you said, Cain then when we get older please marry me." She spoke, her tone seemed a little distant. Warmth entered Cain's stomach, as the words left his lips without even thinking.
"I will, Jen." and within a few more moments the girl Jen captured his lips with her own, and give him a cherry kiss.

He began to wrapped his arms around her small thin hips pushing them together, their breathing became a little harder, both of them glazed in each other eyes, like in the movies. Neither move, both afraid that this will be a dream. She rested her head on his chest and closed her eyes listening to the rhythm of their hearts combined with each rapid beat. They continued to lay there on the coach, pressing against eachother like life depends on it.

"Jen?" He muttered her name through her hair that tickled his nose, not noticing, the door to the apartment opened wildly, and the shouts and screams of Cain's parents filled the apartment. "I told you not to pay for it!" Screeched Cain's mother, to Cain's father who took off his jacket and hang it on the coat hanger in the hallway. "Well unlike your cold heartless heart, I can't let that homeless man starve!" argued Cain's

29

father. Cain's mother stomped her foot walking into the living room and halt in her place. Her eyes widened at the sight of her son embracing a girl, she let out a horrifying scream that snapped the two teens out in their daydreaming.

Jen pulled out of Cain's embrace fast, sitting on the coach a foot away from Cain. Her face went dark red, Cain scrambled to his back that he's facing his mother. His and Jen's shirt is all messy including their hair. "Cain Heartwell! What the hell are you doing having sex with t-that creature without being married!"

Cain could feel his embarrassment and anger rising up his blood. They weren't having sex, if they were, their clothes would be off. His mother just looking for an outlet for her pervious argument.

Cain father entered the room, catching the last bit of information that was spoken. Jen shook her head violently feeling the tears coming down her eyes, she could feel the heated glares of Cain's parents on her shoulders with a look of disappointment.

She didn't do anything wrong and neither has Cain.

"We not having sex." Cain said angry, "Then why are your clothes like tha-"

"I'm sorry, Mrs. Heartwell, Mr. Heartwell, I think I should go now." She spoken, standing up fast from the coach.

"Jen-" Cain was cut off, from his mother.

'Don't Leave me'

"That would be the best, I'll call your parents." Cain mother said with hatred and very stern. Cain could feel his heart crack with every fast step that Jen took towards the door.

" Goodbye, Cain." She sobbed, she opened the door and ran out barely closing the door behind her.

Cain's heart broke onto the floor like China glass. He knew that he wasn't really going to see her again.

He just watched the love of his life ran out on him because of his parents.
"What the hell are you th-"
"Shut up you selfish attention hogging bitch. Just stop this! You always ruin my chance of happiness! When your unhappy you make my fucking life a bitch! You can't stand me being happy! I freaking hate all of you! You always believe the worse out of us! Jen and I wasn't having sex!" Cain screamed through his few tears that fell from his eyes.

Jen wasn't coming back.
It was all his parents fault.

Cain Heartwell's fear: Afraid of being left behind

Chapter Five: I Wouldn't Let You Go

The sky turned dark and a flash of lightning came across a poor innocent white cloud destroying it. The wind began to push and pull the trees back and forth in a wild pattern. Esmee's hair flew behind her head wildly almost knocking her off balance from her feet. This is just like a tornado, her eyes reached the sky above searching for the source. Nothing met her gaze, but the black sky with lightning above. A chill ran through her nervous system. She could easy imagine the lightning striking her of all places. Her heart speed up and she covered her head helpless, closing her eyes. Her breathing became hard, and then something shook her.

Get yourself together. This isn't a real storm. You and the young man is in great danger. Grab him and go. He found us.

The angels like voice panicked in her mind and almost a million thoughts raced through her head, her feet glued to the ground out of fear. Another wave of lightning flashed in the sky and the ground began to rubble. Esmee took in a deep breathe, then the wind became stronger. Cain's body seemed to float in the air, its like someone is pulling him..."No!" Esmee gasped out, thrown herself on top of Cain's body, in which he flinched hard.

The two of them went straight back to the park ground due to their combined weight. She crunched tight on Cain's shirt, her knuckles harden and turned red. This wasn't normal. Something fishy is happening to her and Cain and she doesn't know what it is. She shut her eyes close feeling the extra pull the wind is doing, trying it's best to carry them both up.

'I'm so sorry!' Esmee slammed her hips straight into Cain's stomach, and they jerked back down to the earth. They need to get out of here, but it's impossible. The wind and the storm are the work of the supernatural...and it seems its after Cain.

Esmee looked at Cain sleeping painful face- "I wouldn't let you go, I promise." Esmee promised, her head began to hurt and even through she was a bit confuse of what is happening she wouldn't let anything bad happen to Cain anymore in her care.

The wind suddenly stopped and then heavy footsteps can be heard in a distance of them both.

"aren't that sweet? Protecting your boyfriend, aren't we?" a dark voice can be heard, and Esmee's blood frozen in place.

She felt great evil...She felt it coming from him.
Who is he?
Kaden...He's one of the powerful demon in the demon releam...be careful

The angels like voice fed Esmee the information she wanted to know right off the bat. She looked up at this Kaden person. He has dark raven hair with blackish red eyes within them was indeed no signs of any human part.

He kept on walking and with each step closer Esmee could feel his power and her soul in her body jerked upward.

"W-What do you want?" Esmee spatted out, not moving an inch from Cain, like many humans would of done already, sensing his person.

Kaden smirked in amusement. This lowly human is either brave or stupid.
"Beside you dead? Hand the man over." His voice was cold with a hint of amusement.
Esmee eyes narrowed, even if she just witness his power a few minutes ago she wouldn't back down from her promise.

She grabbed a rock from the ground and threw it at Kaden whom merely ducked his head without much effort.

"No! Stand back!"

"Foolish, I really don't have time for this crap." Kaden stated, raising two of his hands in front of his face, and four claws on each hand slashed out of his skin, like the man off of X-Men.

He was advancing towards them...She have to do something...

A picture of a cross appeared in her hand with a full name, and she knew that the voice just heard her plead.

"Your Kaden Slade! You were killed here aren't you!" Esmee bellowed, making Kaden stopped in his tracks a mere 100 feet away, an emotion that is so foreign is shown in his eyes, before it disappeared clearly the next few moments, but none the less, Esmee caught it.

"So you know my name, girl." He muttered, his blades of his claws doubled in size. At least she stalled him for some time. "I'll make sure you will regret it when I slash you piece by piece." He growled out, but before he could do anything, a shot of a pistol can be heard, and Esmee felt her body jerking backward, by the sudden push by the supposed to be passed out man.

Cain held his pistol aiming it at Kaden, his other hand holding his side weakly, his face twisted in both pain and anger.

"Miss. Lock, please stand aside and let me handle this thing." His voice was painful, Kaden hand flew forward catching the recent bullet that Cain shot.

"I-Impossible." the word left Esmee lips from the side, and then Kaden laughed insane. His claws pulled part as he laughed in the sky, "You believe you still can defeat me Heartwell? You are more foolish that I think. Neither of you can beat me-"

"But I can." a strong angels like voice said from above, Kaden stopped laughing

34

looking at the figure with a look. Esmee and Cain did the same. It was a girl with long flowing blonde hair. She has bright brownish blue eyes. Her huge white wings flapped open as she glided down from the sky above. Her feet was bare, and she wore a white dress, the signature for angels everywhere.

"You again Diamond?" Kaden growled out through his teeth at the angel as she placed her bare feet onto the old concrete of the ground below.

Cain knew this angel...She was the one who saved him.
Esmee awed in amazement. Their IS a world like them.

"Kaden, I'm sure you have better things to do than pacing around this sight." Diamond snarled to Kaden, bright white light came out of her thin perfect shaped body. Kaden closed his eyes, feeling his claws sinking back into his skin. He growled angry to himself. Diamond rose her right hand to the right and suddenly an old style door appeared. A portal for demons. "If you're not going then I'll make you." She swung her arms back and forth, and suddenly the door opened widely and a blast of wind entered the area, pulling Kaden towards the open door to the demon releam.

He didn't say anything, he didn't even struggle against the strong wind that is carrying him off and this surprised Diamond. He is indeed plotting something, when the last inch of Kaden's body entered through the door, the said door fast fade away.

Cain fell onto his back and Esmee still stared at the angel.
"You..You tell me whats going on!" Esmee shouted at the angel and the angel face twisted in disgust at the girl's attitude, but what can she expect from a human that just experience something totally supernatural.

Diamond, ignored Esmee's question and looked down at Cain.

"I already healed your major wounds. Can you still walk?" She demanded.

Cain scowled, and he nodded his head, sitting back up.

"Good." She turned to Esmee.

"I explain everything at his house."

Cain expression turned annoyed,

Bossy angel.

Chapter Six: Don't be Afraid

It was nighttime all of a sudden that Esmee almost blinked in confuse as Cain got up to his own two feet almost falling down onto his knees once more. She glanced at his face it was covered in some unknown emotions of a mask. Is he in pain? Is he hurting? Is he mad? or is he sad? He struggled trying to straight out his coat the best he could, but none the less he still looked like someone had beaten the crap out of him. Esmee moved towards him in hopes to help him, but was stopped when a cold pale white hand went on her shoulders, Diamond leaned by her ear.

"There is something I need to talk about with you alone when we reached his house, something important." Diamond whispered in her ear, and a chill through her body. Esmee barely nodded her head when Cain looked at them with an annoyed expression on his once not bruise face.

"So?"

He walked forward a small bit, his legs felt heavy with each step. He was beyond worn out for his human body.

then Esmee realized something, 'Why his house?'

"We are not talking the portal. It takes too long between time and space." Diamond explained, and Esmee eyebrow risen, "Then we going to walk?" She asked and Diamond almost laughed out loud at that suggestion. Cain shook his head at Esmee's stupidly at moments like this. Why couldn't this girl thinks for once?

Diamond looked at Esmee like a baby, "No, Lock. We are flying. Humans have buses, cars, trucks, bikes, and walk with their legs, angels have portals and wings to fly to their location." Diamond explained to Esmee, and she nodded dumbly at her explanation before her skin went pale at the sudden realizing that she has to fly.

What if she fall? What if someone attacked them in the air? Kaden could come back for them. She surely couldn't fly but something in Diamond's look says otherwise in away that she couldn't understand.

She is afraid.

"F-Flying?"

Diamond nodded her head and then her huge white feather wings, stretched out widely.

"Grab ahold, and hold on tight." Diamond said and Esmee climbed on her right wing, crunching the white feathers through her figures. Her heart beated rapidity. Cain barely got himself on Diamond's left wing without any much panic or fear. He faced worse. He held on to Diamond's edge of her wing, taking a glance at Esmee, his former student, he saw obvious fear. He almost laughed at this. She's afraid of heights but she wasn't afraid of Kaden. That is priceless.

"Ready?"

"Ready"

"R-Ready" when that word left her lips, they were gliding up in the air forward fast. Esmee screamed, her scream radiated through the air above and the ground below. Cain kept a calm face at the take off. Esmee could feel herself beginning to slid down a little on Diamond's wing, and she could feel tears coming down her eyes. She sobbed, tighten ahold of her grip.

"I want it to stop. I want to get off." She silently cried, smashing her face on Diamond's wing. At least she stopped screaming. Her heartbeat went faster and faster with each flap of Diamond wings in the sky. Cain felt bad suddenly. He felt badly for her that is plain and simple. She never fly before judging her reaction now. Cain crawled sideways towards Esmee making sure with each grab is strong and steady. "No moving around!"snapped Diamond from below.

"It's alright Lock. It's just like a rollorcoaster" Cain talked, his voice was very soft, making her looked at him completely. Her face was red and there was still tears coming down her now red blue eyes.

"N-No it isn't. This is a nightmare." She sobbed,
"and why is it a nightmare?"

Esmee laid her head on the wing, her grip haven't loosen it's hold. "T-This is how I lost my mother." She whispered and Cain felt awkward.

"Oh I'm sorry." He muttered, feeling worse now for ever mention anything.

"She loves the sky. She always used a plane to other states, never by car or truck. She loves the sky, the clouds, the stars and the moon above."

"Like this?" Cain found himself saying,

Esmee looked up barely seeing a full moon so close with bright little stars in the night air.

"Yeah, then someday, her plane disappeared off course. No one could find the plane or her." Esmee said sadly, "and this is why you can't stand the thought of flying?" Cain finished for her, and Esmee nodded her head another sob left her lips unwilling. She couldn't believe she just shared her mother's past with him, of all people!

She felt a little better...but then another feeling set in her stomach. It was her fear of rejection.

He will reject her like her step mother had! She turned away from Cain a little, almost scream out in both sadness and sobs at her luck.

"Flying can mean some other things, you know Lock. Flying means freedom. Feel the wind against your skin, do you feel free? I am. The moon and the stars above is beautiful making flying much less dreadful. I felt like this when I was younger when I first flew. Do you love this feeling? Do you love this feeling that your mother loved?"

Esmee looked at Cain in the corner of her eye, and saw a peaceful expression on his face. She felt at ease easy now. She could feel the wind blowing on her back in a soft pattern and a feeling of finally being free entered her mind and head. Cain is right, she did love this feeling of flying, and it only take some talking to make her realized. Her sobs slowly calmed down along with her tears. A smile appeared on her face when she looked up in the night's sky without anymore fear of the what ifs.

"I kind of like this." Esmee muttered, with a small smile on her face, closing her eyes feeling the wind on her skin.

"I told you." Cain laughed, and this was the first time Esmee have ever heard him laughed this close to her before. He's so carefree even in his current state. Diamond shifted downward and back upward in a playing mattered almost making Esmee screamed,

"This isn't funny, Diamond!" Esmee heard herself laughing. She now have a new love for flying. She glanced at Cain once more and she felt even more warmth entered her. She was glad that the wind helped her cool down a bit.

Unknown to the two of them a very special bond had just been formed.

Chapter Seven: Finding Her True Self

The trio stayed in the sky for many minutes before finally reaching their destination. Diamond slowed down ready to dive under like a hawk would do for it's prey. "Hold on tight." Diamond warned the two riders above her wings. Esmee grip tightened on the feathers, her knuckles turned whitish red, and tiny feather came through the cracks of her figures. Cain looked distant, but he kept his hold firm as he can. "Ready?" Cain whispered lowly that she almost didn't hear. Esmee nodded her head, then suddenly as she did so Diamond dived downward. Esmee let out a terror and fearful screeched that radiated in the night sky, as they are flying towards the earth's ground. Her eyes shut close and her hands began to slid downward at the impact of the wind trying to pick her up from Diamond's back. She was going to fall! She will fall!

Then a strong warmth hold came around her shoulders, pulling her body downward to Diamond. She almost fell asleep at the sudden warmth, but finally realizing where she's at, she opened her eyes only to met the rushing ground below. She let out another scream and Diamond's body twisted and began to spin. She felt dizzy, almost letting go. "We almost there, hold on for a little longer." Cain growled out through his teeth, trying to keep his hold tight.

She was met with apartment complexes...This is where Cain lives at and at this moment when Esmee's heart beated faster she knew they weren't going to stop... The building came closer and closer, still no sign of halting.

'STOP!" She screeched and with a huge boom a cloud of golden dusk met the atmosphere. The particles of the golden dusk fell onto the apartment building spreading everywhere.

.~.

The golden dusk began to formed into a human being inside Cain's apartment complex. When the dusk finally ended its transformation, Esmee appeared. She coughed heavy, placing her hand over mouth, falling over the coffee table in the middle of the said room.

"Oww why didn't anyone tell me this?" She muttered to herself, rubbing her back. She was confuse yes. She didn't even know where and what just happened. The room was dark and she placed her hand on the coffee table, helping herself up.

No sign of any life...

"Mr. Heartwell? Angel?" She called out, but nothing met her but silence of the empty room, void of all life.

'Need to find the light switch, and then the others.' Esmee thought to herself forming a half plan. She walked slowly through out the room, barely dodging a large object. She stopped a few feet from the door, when suddenly golden glowing dusk appeared before her.

It quickly transformed into a human being. This wasn't Cain, but Diamond herself. Esmee breathe a sign of relief when suddenly the room light came on automatically, revealing everything. She was indeed in Cain's living-room. The coffee table was crooked in the middle of room, due that Esmee tripped over it. In front of the table was a huge flat scene tv, and behind the table was a comfy looking sofa.

"Where's Cain?"

The words slipped her lips without much thought. Diamond waved it off without much worry,

"He's fine, just sleeping his pain off in the next room." Diamond said, then pointing at sofa rudely.

"Please take a seat, I have something to explain to you tonight." She said, before waving her left hand, the door behind her slammed shut, and the window in the left corner shut close, covering it with the brown long curtain.

Esmee nodded her head, remembering what Diamond said at the park. She took a seat on the sofa, and Diamond walked in front of it, barely pushing the coffee table away.

"I'm Diamond, one of the heaven's angel that is send down to help keep the balance between the demons, angels, spirits and humans. The demon that attacked you is one of the powerful demon in his releam. The reason why I could defeat him so easy, is because he's weak in the human releam in any sunlight." Diamond gave Esmee a crash course in what to come.

She stayed quiet.

Her hands were on her knees,

and for once in her mind she was actually thinking.

This must be true.

The proof was staring at her in the face and already proven. Her face grew pale..

"W-Why are they after Cain." Esmee muttered, crunching her hands into a pair of fist.

Diamond sighed loudly, "Because Cain is a Supernatural Offical in this area. With him out of the way, its be easier to reached their goal." She explained,

"and..and is he a human?" Esmee refereed to Cain,

and Diamond nodded her head.

"Yes, he's is human. Humans could only be Supernatural Officers. He was born with the sight, just like you." Diamond walked back and forth, her wings are back into her back, she looked more human now.

"Have you wonder what happened to your mother, Esmee?"

Sadness, flow through Esmee's body and she nodded her head.

"She's plane crashed somewhere unknown." Esmee said sadly, looking anywhere but at Diamond. Diamond stared at Esmee hard,

"No. She's alive."

Esmee head jerked up fast with surprised.

Diamond waved her hand nonchantly to her right, then an image of a woman appeared floating. She was all dark...Her aqua...She worn a black dress. Her darkish black hair hung up high over her head. Her eyes were red, and she also worn bright red lipstick with high heels...A modernly day slut in the human releam. On her back was a pair of two huge black bat wings, and Esmee frozen. Her blood ran cold and her skin paled.

This was her mother...

"N-No! That's not her." She denied picturing, her last memory of her mother in her mind. She looked much more kind with always a smile on her tan face.

"This is her indeed. She's a demon from the demon releam. Seven-teen years ago she ranaway from the demon releam, tired of being captive against her will. She ran to the human world, easiest place to hide. She transformed into a human being sealing her powers away. She was ordinary. Then one day, she found this human man. Your father, she fell in love fast. When she had you, she was happy. Five years, later she took a plane towards New York city, her family came and took her and the plane away towards the demon world." Diamond told Esmee, her mother history, leaving out something important.

"I-Impossible! My mom is human!" Esmee screamed, in hope of convincing herself more that her mom is still the kind human mother when she was five.

Diamond walked closer to Esmee, with an emotionless look.
"There is only one proof, Lock and your it."

then suddenly Esmee's world seemed to spin around back began to sting and the human flesh began to tear up, She screamed. She screams in pain and for help, but she knew no one would come and safe her. Cain was asleep, a deep one.

Two huge black bat wings popped behind her back, her heart hurts against her chest. Rejecting the creature she is becoming.

Diamond just stood there and watch.
"This is for your own good Lock. Your a Half Demon by your mother genres."

The pain stopped, and Esmee limped to the flat scene tv, that shows little of her reflections.
She was indeed a half demon..
Her black wings shown her it.

Dark thoughts seemed to resurface.

'Why did she truly left?'
'Why her step mother rejected her'
'Why has her father blamed her for his divorce from that witch of a wife'
'Why no one told her what she is,'
They all deserve to die!

Dark aqua surrounded Esmee and she almost roared. Diamond stood her ground watching Esmee being engulfed with evil and dark thoughts due of her demon transformation.

'If her mother left her when she was five, and still married her real father...then thats means...her step father is..is her adoptive father! Her real father gave her up!'

Esmee wanted to smash or crush anything in sight now, her former human self began to disappear in thin air in the subcontance of her brain.

'This means her whole life is a WHOLE lie!'

Esmee held her forehead, her head banged in ache.
"This is your trueself. You cannot change it! Your a half demon. You are naturally evil! This is you!" Diamond stated harshly at Esmee, whom is now began to float in air, almost reaching the ceilling.

'No, Esmee. Don't give in. This isn't you at all.' Esmee mind has spoken to her softly, and her eyes popped opened in half rage.

"Yes it is!" screeched Esmee. She was in deep physically and mentally pain.
"That woman doesn't know you. She can't tell you if this you. Only you can see if this is you. This is your choice. You can choose your destiny." Her human mind plead.

"Your evil, therefore creatures like you should be dead!" Diamond screamed at Esmee to increase her innersuffering.

'Kill her. Kill the witch. See how much pain she's giving you? Make her suffer the same." The demon part talked evilly,

"Demons cannot remain well forever. They will slip. Just like your mother!" Diamond kept on poking her,

"Please Esmee, dear. This demon isn't you. This is you. This nice human girl."

The room blinded with white light when Esmee floated back to her feet almost falling over. Her wings went back inside her back and she felt super sleepy.

Diamond stared in awed. She fought her demon half and won slightly.

46

"I want sleep." She muttered, her eyes drifted close and Diamond grinned.

"Very well, but this is the start of you and Cain test through your dream." Diamond

voice faded in Esmee's mind, when she finally fell asleep. Her body fell to the floor,

worn out.

Chapter Eight: Don't Fight Back

The sun almost blinded her when she rubbed her eyes confused. Where was she? She

remembered falling asleep, into a deep one. A blurry image of Diamond entered her

mind, she touched her forehead and felt her soft skin...Wait..No bandage or scar? She

looked behind her back quickly, and saw no pair of black bat wings, as the recent

events trembled in her mind.

She quietly walked, fear and confuse entered her with each and passing step within the

gates of hell school. She was at school... She was also in her school uniform wearing

her messenger bag...She didn't remember getting dressed in them at all. Something is

totally wrong, when she passed the table, where the staff of the school checked the

students for weapons, uniform and stuff like that before walking in the main entrance.

Her eyes glanced everywhere to the double doors that onto the left of her and a huge

opening to the Court Yard on her right. It all seemed normal. Nothing out of

place..except..There was a girl with dark brown hair with chocolate brown eyes

waiting by the red locker. She looked at Esmee and a smile formed on her face.

"Hey Esmee! Finally showing up before the bell." She laughed, halfway jogged

besides Esmee and they turned a right to the courtyard that is packed with students of

all grades hanging out.

"Aly?" The shock ran through her and she could still felt the leftover anger of

47

yesterday coming back to her full force, but she was able to hold it back at the moment.

"Yes?"

"What's today's date?"

"It's Wednesday, silly."

Esmee stopped walking completely.

"W-Wednesday?" She stumbled over her word and Aly nodded her head, holding to her books while she did so. A worry look appeared on her face,

"Yes it is. What's wrong?"

Esmee shook her head, "Nothing." She replied, walking to an abandon red picnic table, setting her bag down. Aly did the same, and took a seat on top of the table. Esmee sit down beside her bag on top. They watched as the students filed up walking through the gate then splitting up to their location.

The sky was so clear and it was almost like Diamond or any demon have ever exist. A few teachers walked passed the halls and disappearing to their left towards the portables classrooms.

"Are you sure, your okay? You been acting strange." Aly stated from her observation.

"I'm fine. I'm always fine." Esmee almost snarled out, remembering all those times that she had been suffering, and no one asked her if she was ever alright.

A figure that Esmee knew so well turned left towards the teaching portables that

Esmee almost jumped out of her seat. Cain would know what happened. She could

talk to him, but something within her head told her its wasn't a good idea to do so.

Esmee jumped down from the table, swinging her bag over her shoulder.

"Where are you going?"

Aly asked, getting down from the table.

"I just remember something, I'll meet you in the library. Okay."

Esmee ran off after Cain leaving Aly speechless.

~.~

"Mr. Heartwell?" Esmee called, just as she just a few feet from the young man, whom

looked very tired. He worn a dark green polo shirt with dark blue jeans. He hold his

own black message bag with his fingers weakly and very tired. Cain stopped walking

in front of one building and he turned his head at the person who called his name. He

barely smiled,

"Yes, Miss. Lock? Do you need something?" He asked and Esmee just stood there and

gapped at him like a fish out of water. He acts like his oldself when she was in school.

Not the Cain in the park or the one flying with her. This one is different.

She lost her words to speak the truth on why she wants to talk to him when suddenly

she changed her mind suddenly.

"No not really, Mr. Heartwell. I just want to say good morning. Good morning sir."

Esmee said, with a mock salute. He laughed lowly at Esmee's playfulness. "Good

morning to you." He relied to Esmee, "I have to go now, have to finish those lesson

49

plans." He suddenly said awkwardly, realizing something himself, disappearing in the building they both stop walking to.

He left Esmee alone... Something seemed to jerk in her mind when suddenly she could feel an angry aqua behind her. "So this is where you have been Lock! This isn't something important isn't it? Stalking, Mr. Heartwell is just sick!" Aly growled out marching towards Esmee, who looked at her like a demon disgust. Aly seriously had a split personalty. Esmee wasn't actually stalking Cain. She did have something to talk to him about, but she has no more classes with him this year made it hard for her to speak alone with him.

"I'm not stalking." Esmee snarled out at Aly, matching Aly's anger with her own. Let see whom going to win at this.

Aly forced out a harsh laugh.

"Sure its isn't. What do you call a person whom just stand there and stare at the building for thirty minutes?"

"Aly...Your attitude is pissing me off. Shut the hell up!" screeched Esmee in rage. How dare her jumped on her like this! Who does she think she is anyway to do this?

"My attitude pissing you off? You pissing me off, freak! What friend you are, ditching me like that!"

Esmee's hand's went straight to the collar of Aly's red shirt and pushed her against the building with such inhuman strength. She wanted to beat the crap out of her supposed to be friends. She was almost blinded against her rage not noticing that they were being watched by their fellow classmates from a distance.

Esmee suddenly let go when a sudden wave of sadness and loneliness slammed into her. She loosen her grip on Aly's collar, who just glared at her with a hateful look. Esmee head hung low not looking at Aly's face at all.

"I thought we were friends? Why are we fighting like this?" Esmee almost choked out. Aly expression stayed the same.

"Then we aren't."

Esmee let go of Aly only to met a punch to the face, knocking Esmee to the ground. Aly stood over her fallen form. She picked up her right leg and kicked Esmee in her stomach making her scream on impact. She rolled away from Aly the best she could, tears forming in her blue eyes. She could hear cheering of her classmates around her-"Fight. Fight. Fight"

"Stop crying!" Aly snapped, kicking her on her back, Esmee rolled to her front and small sobs slipped her lips only making Aly madder.

"Get up and fight me you coward! Fight me!" She turned into a rapid fast punches and kicks to Esmee whom just laid there almost defenceless. Esmee tried to protect her head, but with each kick and punch she let out a painful scream. 'Fight back. You can easy beat her up!' A dark voice whispered in her mind and it was tempted, but no. She wasn't going to fight back. She wasn't going to fight a friend. "Please stop." Esmee whimpered out, "Like hell I would." Then the beatings stopped, when suddenly a strong grip pushed Aly on her back really heavy.

"Is that the way to treat a friend?" The harsh voice told Aly. She knew this voice. Esmee rolled onto her stomach, she wasn't going to let him see how much pain she was in nor the mess she looked like now. She wasn't bleeding, thank goodness for that, but she was indeed bruised in most places on her body.

"She's not a friend of mine." Aly spatted,

"And why not? Just because she walked here? Go to the office, if I find out you aren't there in ten minutes, I'll make sure you be expelled." He hissed at Aly, and Aly nodded her head mad before stalking off. The classmates split up aswell with the words 'awww'

"Miss. Lock? Can you get up?" Mr. Heartwell smoothly said, and Esmee shook her head. Her body hurts so bad that she couldn't move at all.

Cain sighed under his breathe. He almost didn't believe that people would do that to one another. He pushed his arms under Esmee's back and then legs and with a honest effort he picked her up. He have to admit. Esmee was alittle heavy, but he wouldn't dare to tell her that. Esmee leaned her head downward looking up at the sky, which is turning blackish gray for some unknown reason.

"We're going to the office and call your house. For your father to pick you up." He told her, carrying her to the office, passing up many students who looked at them strange.

Then one of her black bat wings popped out behind her back, her eyes widened in horror. She watched Cain's face twisted up in loathe. He suddenly let her go, making her fall on her back in pain. Her second wing, came out at the landing.

"Y-Your a demon." He stumbled out,

"Half demon" Esmee corrected him, only feeling that he's not going to take it well at all.

Without much warning, time stopped and he fished out his pistol that she saw at the park that he shot at Kaden with.

Her eyes began to tear up again.

"You wouldn't.." She whispered out crying that is all she could ever do.

"Your a demon, therefore need to be perish." He stated coldly pulling the trigger of his pistol.

POP!

Esmee flapped her wings back and forth, barely dodging the bullet when she suddenly flew clumsy in the air a few 10 feet above Cain, and she was suddenly thankful that the this is a open school.

She felt betrayed and hurt.

She felt rejection and loneliness.

The evil part of her will consume the good part of her in time. Time unfrozen, and many students stopped walking and pointed at her with loathe.

"Freak!" cries of the awful word circled around the area.

She just wanted to get the heck away from here.

She looked down below watching Cain, hurrying and got rid of his pistol.

"I trusted you." She mouthed to him, only seeing that he turned away from her automatically.

~.~

Esmee woke up due that someone is actually poking her side of her body. She opened her eyes meeting Cain's tired ones.

"You have a nightmare. Are you okay?"

Esmee nodded her head sadly, feeling the wetness under her eye-lids. She's crying in her sleep! Cain moved his hand towards Esmee back, wanting to hug her, to somewhat comfort her but she backed away, seeing his hand.

Hurt, shown on his face before he masked it back up easy.

Esmee seemed to find her voice, "Where's Diamond?"

"She left hours ago. I just woke up myself...The dream we have was a test. It looks like you barely passed." He said softly, standing up from the sofa, throwing an old blanket on Esmee before he moved to the door.

"What time is it?"

"2am, night." He left.

Suddenly a certain realization came upon her shoulders. She had spend the night at Cain's house. She didn't called her step father. Oh lord, he will surely be pissed at her in the morning.

She closed her eyes slowly trying to erase the hurt and stress she is feeling. She touched her forehead, and the rough feeling of a bandage met her.

Chapter Nine: Mother and Daughter

Ivory Lock looked out of her bedroom window with a fix expression on her face. It had been many years since her family came and took her away from the human world...Took her away from her husband and daughter. For many days she would long to see them again, but with each attempt that she made to visit them over the years was ruined by her father. "Your going to take over the Demon World in a few months. You can't go around and hanging out with humans." He told her, not knowing she had indeed married one and gave birth to a half demon.

So now she's at the age of 35 in human years, sitting all alone waiting for the man that her father decided to marry her, which is completely unfair. She's an adult in this world too. She could pick out her own husband. The human one that she grew to love so much...but yet she should of known that this would happened. She could pick out her own clothes. A long black gothic dress, who want to wear that? Not her.

Her heart tugged, and she felt the emotional pain that she tried to hide away for so long came back. How's her daughter doing? How's her husband doing? She almost cried at that thought..No when she become Queen of the demon world she would kick her demon husband out and then go see her love ones. Who going to stop a Queen anyway? No one.

The plane that her family took still laid in the dungeon of their castle. The humans on board had quickly become their slaves or servants. This isn't Ivory's choice. She couldn't do anything about this.

The doors opened in her room, revealing her father and another young man that she already distaste. Her father was in his demon form and so was the young man. Their bats like wings hanged behind them with great power, their eyes shined a crimson red, the feeling of blood lust filled the room.

Her father eyes settled on her in disapproval of her form.
"Ivory, how many times did I told you always to use your demon form? Not your human form." He snarled at his daughter.

Ivory looked at the floor below,
"Sorry father, its a habit." She muttered, her black wings popped out on her back slowly unfolding them wide.

Her father looked at the young man, who held a snake like smile on his face.
"Sorry, about my daughter, Tom. She can be a handful of a time." He told him, and Ivory searched this man character. He looks sinister...All demons does.

"Ivory, this is Tom Foster. He will be your Fiancee."
and with that sentence her whole world almost trembled, before the reality settled in her head.
If her family found out about her own husband and her daughter they would mostly be killed...

A tear slid down her eyes,
She's doing this for them...
She smiled fake at Tom,

"Nice to meet you Tom."

Chapter Ten: It Wasn't Love

She doesn't want to go to school so it wasn't a great surprise when her former History teacher told her to stay or go to her house to get some more sleep, which she happy took his offer, before he left for work.

She felt bruised almost beyond repair, that she struggled with herself to her own choice of telling Cain about her race. What happened if he reacted like he did in her dream? Cain does have a deep hatred of demons beyond repair. He would hate her, even if he had a kind and gentle personality within him.

'She left hours ago. I just woke up myself...The dream we have was a test. It looks like you barely passed.'

But what about him?

The clock on the wall read 10:00am in the morning, making her groaned, on the sofa under the old smelly blanket. She should wake up and go home now, even through her step father would most likely abuse her when she returned, but she found herself asking herself, what's the use. Her whole life was a lie.

It was definitely mess up. She snuggled back into the streets, wanted all of her trouble to be gone. A small golden particles started to built up in front of the sofa, and she almost sworn. Not her again. Not Diamond. She doesn't want to face the bossy angel yet, but it was too late, the particles already formed into the said angel.

When her body is fully formed, she smiled down on Esmee's form on the sofa.
"So, hows the rest?" She asked, and Esmee groaned at her and she frowned.

"now wake up, sit up, there is some other things we need to talk about."

Diamond for once said smooth.

Esmee sit up on the soft sleepy, trying to regain her focus. Her blood boiling mad at her for disturbing her sleep and rest.

"As you already know, that the dream you have its a test."
"Yeah Cain, told me."

"Then you should know he failed." Diamond said sadly, watching Esmee's expression closely, sawing the confuse and shock look on her face.
"W-What is his test?"

Diamond looked away,

"To not shoot you or harm you when you tell him your race. He pulled out the pistol automatically and you know." Diamond said, and Esmee could felt her world falling apart right there. Cain didn't even pause before pulling the trigger on her. She should of expected that. She didn't really know Cain except a few run ins, and this.

A dark depressing aura surrounded Esmee,

"I really don't have nothing anymore." Esmee whispered, a bit of envy slammed into her. Why couldn't she be like a normal kid? Why had her mother been taken away? Why had Aly turned on her? Why had her real father gave her mother and her away so easy?

'It wasn't love.'

The obvious answer came to her head. Her real father never really love her mother or her. He was being kind and pretending to love them, because he felt like he have to.

A few tears slid down her eyes, what should she do now?

Diamond patted her back softly,

"The man you saw at the park and fought is Kaden Slade. He's trying to take over the demon world and for him to do that he have to get your mother. To get your mother, he needs you." Diamond explained the current problem, feeling like it was finally time for her to know.

She bit her lip, even through she hate the fact that her mother is a demon. That she have her blood, but for some reason she felt like she have a duty she must preform.

This short time she had finding it out, she almost know what she should do. She must find her mother before Kaden and his lackys ever find her or her mother.

"I want to find my mother." Esmee whispered.

"Are you sure? It's not going to be easy." Diamond warned. Esmee haven't even master her demon powers yet and it would be foolish for her to rush into this.

"Even through, mother is a demon. She doesn't deserve this. Dad didn't love her and he let her go easy without a fight. I refuse to be like him."

Diamond smiled at Esmee, 'Good girl'

"Fine, when you reached in the demon world, your powers will become stronger. Just remember who you are." Diamond said, pulling out a few scrolls from her small pouch on her hip.

"These are a few old maps, and a demon info. Scroll that I always kept on me. You can borrow them for the time being. Time change the moment you reach the demon world"

Esmee looked at Cain's apartment, with a sad look on her face.

"Can I leave a note?" She whispered, and Diamond nodded her head. "Hurry."

And so Esmee left a note for Cain,

Dear Mr. Heartwell,

Thank you for everything, I'm going to visit my aunt's house to get a break from this stuff. I need a fresh air. I wouldn't be back for awhile.

Your former student,

Friend,

Esmee Lock.

Esmee placed the note on the coffee table. Diamond summoned a portal, golden gate.

"The moment you walk in those gates, your in the demon world. Good luck."

Esmee pushed opened the gate, bright light almost blinding her.

Chapter 11: Destined to Die

She didn't know what happened now. The last she remembered was that she pass through the gate and then she blacked out for some reason. Maybe the gate attacks the demon blood within her, causes her human side to faint. That's the only logical reason that her brain could think of. She crunched her hands on the ground, not feeling the grass on her figure tips, but something sticky, a horrible scent reached her noise and her face twisted in disgust. Yuck! Gross! It smells like the dead..

She looked underneath her to the supposed to be ground and saw the dark crimson of blood...blood and the hard surface of animal bones. Her face paled and a shiver moved through her hand, as she tried to stand up on her legs, but got back down by the stickiness of the red liquid below, holding her down...

For this liquid, so many must of being killed.

She lifted her right hand, only to be pulled back down once more.

A sigh left her lips, she need to get out of this fast.

'transform' a small voice in her head whispered, her bat wings could easy picked herself off the ground and fly in the air.

Fly?

The word alone made her scared...but wasn't she already over this? Without Cain or Diamond here to guide her, she doesn't have the will to do it on her own.

Her mind went fuzzy, as the scent of blood clouded up her scent of smell and her brain. She could hear her heart pound rapidly against her chest louder and louder ready to jump right out. A small strange black birds flew over her, screeching at one another-"CRAW!" before flying fast apart from each other.

The sky above was dark black as the lightning escaped the black clouds above covering any light except the white flashes of lightning in the sky.

One of the black birds flew back lower staring at her, eyes narrowed. The bird opened it's beck and suddenly huge wind escaped it's beck and headed down toward's Esmee.

"Human!" it screeched loudly overhead.

Her human defenses reacting, closing her eyes waiting for the incoming slashes, but she stopped her right eye lid from closing. Wait...She can't wait for danger like this, so easy. Diamond warned her and she accepted it anyway.

Two small black bat wings popped out of Esmee's upper back and she blinked at the size.

It was bigger in her world, but enough of that. The red liquid stickled together to her wings, and a bitter feeling entered her stomach, her human side telling her something, but her demon side is ignoring it.

She flapped opened her wings, and she shoot up in the sky suddenly dodging the wind that the bird thrown her way before. The bird looked at Esmee studded, it opened up it's beck once more-

"Demon!" before flying off.

Esmee eyes looked down at the ground below, her wings flapping uneven. The sudden full sight made her stomach upset. The whole ground was covered with the crimson liquid. Pieces of bones of any creature or animal maybe human was sticking out of the liquid.

'Disgusting'

She refused to let her own feet to touch the ground below anymore. She looked in front of her, instead of the lightning, she saw a castle in the far distance, built on some rocks. She flapped her wings once more, deciding to head to the castle. She's here for once reason. One reason only for now and its her mother.

Now how can she fly forward?

Diamond made it looked so easy...

Esmee leaned her body sideways, and she suddenly felt herself flying slowly forward.

Oh the joys of flying.

"Help me! Help!" a cried can be heard down below, and her eyes looked down and saw a few shadowly figures gliding on the red liquid, struggling. One of the figure is shaped like a dog and the other shaped like a human being.

Once again the urge of wanted to help went through Esmee, but not as strong as before. Her demon side pushing her to go forward and ignore those creatures. It could be a trap, for someone like her, but then her naive side is telling her to help them.

They aren't alive anymore. They are creatures of the dead known as ghosts or spirits.

Even knowing this, Esmee couldn't help but to fly down.

"Is their something I could help you with?" She asked, and their cries stopped. They looked up at Esmee with dark black holes as eyes.

There frowns turned into grins, and suddenly the red liquid flew upward like a rope and around her ankle pulling her downward into the blood red abyss.

Esmee eyes widened as her wings flapped repeatedly upward trying to escape but the hold on her right ankle was strong and firm.

"Yes your blood!"

The red liquid has a mind of it's own, pulling her downward second by second even through she was trying her best to fly upward. Her wings aren't strong enough, the two shadow figures fade into a black sparkled mist.

It was a trap!

How could she fell for it...Oh her human side did.

'You need to let go of that weakling.' her demon side told her about her human side. Esmee shook her head, no. She's not going give that part up. That is the only part is still true about her at all. The red liquid pulled downward harder.

"Your a stubborn one, aren't you?" The voice was now deeper and dark like, the hold began to hurt. She gasped, but she didn't give up even through her wings are getting tired of flapping upward, while being pulled back down.

A few visions came through her all at once.

The poor demons, angels, humans, creatures and animals that formed this monster is still there...Their souls aren't put to rest yet, of what they had become.

She flapped her wings slower and let herself being dragged down.

Her eyes watered, at the visions of the sudden death these people got when they first appeared in the demon world.

Oh the cruel deaths by their own.

One of her many teardrops fell into the crimson liquid that held her down.

"You don't deserve this at all." The sentence left her lips without her noticing it making the grip on her feet halt in the progress in pulling her down. Her tears mixed with the blood below, making it bubbling,

"You know what they did to us? So you know what it like to be like this?" The monster became even more angry.

The monster isn't one, but one of many who had formed this being.

Esmee didn't answer at the monster's question..Just because she didn't have the answer for once. She didn't know how it felt. So why should be any different for her to be here? If they were killed on the spot, she will be too. It's the only way to keep the balance of hatred alive.

Diamond send Esmee to her death with fake little hopes.

"Your going to be one of many of us-"

"Please stop this! What will this prove anyway? So what they did to you was not right, I understand your pain and suffering. But why carry this out to many others that came here with dreams? Why are you crushing the dreams of many of your people because of something that someone did to you all! Why punish the living? Just why!"

The monster hold on her ankle tightened and in which some of her blood came leaking through and fell right into the monster. Esmee yanked her feet upward-

"They don't deserve to keep living while we all down here is trapped with no way out." The monster snapped, and suddenly Esmee wings gave out and she fell into the abyss of the red liquid.

"CAIN!" Esmee screamed out, her mouth filled with the red liquid which is pulling her downward to drowned.

She struggled upward once more with the small ability of her's to swim.

"DIAMOND!" but no one was coming to help her. The strange reality hit her like a pound of bricks. She is destined to stay here and die...die...die.

with the last of her strength she screamed out "MOM!"

and she went under. Her eyes closed and her lungs filled with the disgusted liquid.

Her tears mixed with the blood once more.

She had fallen.

She's dying and there was nothing she could do about it.

Chapter 12: Be Free

She saw red, just pure blood red. Will anyone come to save her? Her lungs began to filled with the inelegant liquid and her stomach twisted ready to vomit the stuff out. She shut her eyes closed, as more of the liquid gleeful entering inside her nose than her mouth. Her batlike wings twitched in the sticky crimson liquid, tiny bones struck her sides.

"Now I'll make you pay for what they had done to us all." the monster roared in her mind but still she couldn't escape. The oxygen that her human body runs off is getting lower and lower to the point of suffocation.

She doesn't deserve this.

No one does.

She can't die here and with a loud whined her body glowed dark black. Huge amount of purplish wind surrounded her, pushing the red liquid away rather easy.

The ground where she now stood upon was dried covered in animals decay. The red crimson liquid flew around her blinding her for the real sight of the demon realm.

Esmee's hair stood straight upward her eyes opened slowly, as to why she didn't felt anything much anymore or why she isn't dead yet. The purple wind was her own demon aura, protecting her...

The sticky goo loosened it's hold on her wings, feeling the strength coming back very slow, she flapped them apart and easy the goo is gone and her wings are freed. She could maybe fly out now.

Flapping them over and over a small spark of hope went through her mind like someone had pulled a trigger from a pistol.

Her feet lifted from the ground and slowly she floated higher and higher in the air. The wind brush her wet hair up and she felt a chill past her hair line.

"No!" a huge red rope like whip swung into the purple wind with such force that she almost flew backward completely.

She is almost out of here and when she is way up in the air the monster wouldn't be able to get her.

The purple wind fade away just as she's up 200 feet from the ground. The red liquid smashed around over and over and within the crimson liquid was shaped with hundreds of faces mixed with agony, screaming.

"Helpppp" They cried once more to her, but she remained unfazed this time, even through her heart is sinking second by second at the sight and their screams. This is a trap to lure her back in.

This wasn't going to trick her a second time around.

The souls of many beings beneath her was horrified, but she found her courage to move forward, to fly forward.

These souls are beyond in need of help. There was nothing she could do about it, not now anyways.

"I come back soon and set you all free!" She screamed down at the pack of souls that formed one being, a monster that could barley be recognized.

She flew uneven forward, unnoticed the crimson liquid below her began to disappear and fade into tiny red sparkles of dusk and into the dark black sky above.

They were free and Esmee don't even know it yet.

It had been a week since he last saw her. A painful week that he haven't see her bright face and glowing energy. Cain placed his hand on his forehead, looking down at the note that Esmee left behind a week ago today, rereading the words.

She should be back already. The seeing the dead shouldn't have scared her this bad. A guilty feeling settle in his stomach, maybe it was the flying.

Maybe she's still scared of it and hate being around the person who was with her or the cause of it.

Maybe she had indeed ranaway? The supernatural stuff could easy scare off a normal human being. A groaned, left his lips as he put on his coat, buttoning up the five buttons on his top. He shouldn't be thinking of why she left this much. He shouldn't even care of where she could have gone...

It's not like he like her in a romantic way, its more like in a friendship. The phrase in her letter made an impact on him. 'Your friend'

In someways he was more of a friend to her than any other relationship he have.

She meant something to him, a small part.

When he finished button up his coat and place on his black steel toe boots and place his small pistol in his pocket. The clock over head reminded him of nighttime, 9pm.

It was time for him to make his round around Bunkie now, to see if everything's all right. Nothing out of the normal. It was his job, his main duty given by the head angel Spade. He's the human Supernatural Offical.

Checking, if he have everything in check, he pulled out his hand-

"From the great heavens above let me pass the steps of heaven and take me to the place where need to be protected."

The chant came so easy to him nowdays and suddenly a bright gold gate appeared in front of him. The gates flew wide opened, and bright white light came flashing out almost blinding him.

He placed his right arm in front of his face, shielding. He took a few steps forward and suddenly he began to slid inside the portal. The gates closed behind him and within a few seconds the gate fade away slowly.

Chapter 13: Falling for the Kidnapper

She almost didn't believe on why she almost had let her own life slip between her figures so easy without much of a fight.

Her skin began to take on a darker shade of ivory as her two feet reached the courtyard of the castle.

Her wings folded back into her back suddenly and the dominance of another demon aura came crushing down on her shoulders, making her fall to her knees.

The blood in which she almost drowned by, dried up and the dark gross smell of blood could be smelled by a far distance.

Her joints throbbed with each movement to stand back up to her feet, but failed doing so.

She is a half demon and half human. The demon aura would affected her human side easy, than her demon side.

The castle door opened, downward. A huge brown gate that is covered with unexplainable spikes.

An orange gust of wind surrounded her and then a woman in her late 30's walked in Esmee's vision.

She was beautiful. Her long dark black hair flow straight downward with her bright sparking green eyes, that sharped on contact of her sight.

Her thin pale pink lips grinned upward when her sight met Esmee's.

"Oh hello there dear, how did a kid like you reach here?" the voice was so fake it almost made Esmee vomited.

The fake sweetness in her voice made it obvious that she wasn't wanted here at all.

"eh I flew." Esmee tried the obvious answer till the woman laughed.

"haha yeah right, honey. No demon could fly around the Crimson Lake. You have to be an immortal to survive the journey." She laughed, and Esmee glared at her with dislike.

What other way could she get here from?

She searched her brain of all the times on how Diamond traveled and then Kaden. A portal.

"I'm telling the truth, see the blood on my clothes?" Esmee snarled at the demon. Her laughter died down with a look of realize set on her features.

"Oh, you might want to get washed up then. I'm Elani Star, mistress of the Crimson Castle on the boarder of the Crimson Lake." the demon Elani introduce herself poorly, but yet formally.

Esmee stared dumbfounded.

"My name is Esmee Lock from the demon realm." Esmee sort of lied, but the woman seemed to buy it when she shook head.

"Come along dear, I show you to the washroom."

Elani was plotting something and Esmee doesn't like it.

The two of then walked in silence inside the castle. Inside the castle, was all in the color of red, almost no other color. The scent of blood grew stronger, and Esmee was sure its not coming from her.

The castle seemed to rattle sightly in warning and Esmee seemed a little spook, seeing that Elani casted her a glance-"It's normal. It's the souls of the people who died here"

People=Humans

The way Elani had said people almost slip out of Esmee's mind.

The souls in this place are trapped...

Crimson...She mind as well have a history lesson from one of Diamond's demon scrolls soon.

Elani halted infront of a chamber, small door.

"We're here. If you need anything I'll be in the herot." She waved mindlessly, before disappearing in the cloud of smoke.

Esmee hand touched the wall, letting it chase the outline of the wall feeling...A small sticky liquid stuck to her figure tips. Blood.

She shiver and she felt her feet began to froze on their own accord, but then she shook it off before opening the washroom door carefully as she could.

A small nagging feeling told her to be careful.

Who would let a stranger wondering around the castle?

When she opened the washroom fully, a hand soon came covered her mouth from behind.

"Hello, Lock. Miss me?" A dark familar voice hissed in her ear, making her almost jumped out of her feet.

"Kaden!"

A small memory came through Esmee's mind remembering the day.

She could hear a dark chuckle.

"Right, it's surprised me on how you easy came across my house and to the hands of my sister." Kaden whispered, making her heartbeat a bit faster than normal making her own eyes widened.

Her face heatup, and all she wanted to do was to yell at him on what spell he casted on her now.

"Now your my prisioner, be quiet and everything will be fine."

Esmee struggled, fast opening her bat like wings to put some fast distance between her and her captiver.

But her wings easy break or went back inside her back, when Kaden's iron hold held her down.

She was being kidnapped.

Her heart beat somewhat 90 miles per hour. Who in the right mind will have a crush on there kidnapper?

Maybe he did cast a spell over her to feel like this...To make her less likely to runaway...

Her body then went limp, as her demon form began to disappear within seconds revealing her human form. The weak form she is cursed to be in.

"Your in my world, Lock. My powers are stronger here than the human realm."

Cain...

The part of her that depended on Cain and admire him is starting to fade...to fade in the dark corners of her human mind.

Chapter 14: Don't Forget

Esmee barley glanced at Trace the entire hour. It was no surprise to see him here. He jumped out of a two story window! So it's wasn't a surprise to see him here as a demon. She felt a little hurt that he had deceived her. She didn't know him any long, so it didn't hurt as it should of been.

"Hello, Esmee."

Esmee stayed quiet, avoid looking at him. He was the enemy and therefore should be ignore or killed.

Wow she had indeed somewhat develop Cain's beliefs.

Cain..

Her hands were bonded behind her back, and her feet tied together in the front. She leaned against the wall on her side, breathing somewhat heavier than normal. The room that they thrown her in and the guard that Kaden placed her with is abnormal.

Her human side is weakened by the aura.

He is slowly fading from her mind, she could barley slow the progress of human memory decay down. She only knew Cain by her human form...His smile, his laughter and his voice...They will all be gone, leaving nothing behind but a nameless face.

I wouldn't forget...

She doesn't want this...She still want to remember.

A rule in the demon world: All humans cannot survive.

Its a fact of survival and a basic one at that. Human memories will decay and then the body and lastly the soul. It shouldn't effect Esmee so much through, seeing she's half human and demon.

Kaden explained to her the progress before leaving for who knows where.

The sound of his name made Esmee heartbeat a little harder, no she must remain faithful to her kind. Kaden hurt Cain, and therefore he will pay. Kaden is after her mom, she shouldn't let him near her or whatever.

"So you wouldn't speak to me then or even look at me."

Trace looked at Esmee, who completely stayed emotionless.

"What else is there to talk about? Your friend kidnapped me, and your making sure I can't escape." Esmee muttered darkly under her breath, turning away completely from Trace, who just shrugged his shoulders.

"Well that's life."

"Only if people like you make it like that!" Esmee snarled back and Trace blinked before regaining his own wits.

"All due for humans like-"

The door behind Trace slammed opened up revealing Elani, angry. Her hair is a mess and her makeup ran down her green eyes.

"Will the two of you shut the hell up! I have sensitive hearing and if I hear one more remark you both going to the Crimson Water!"

Her hair stood up wildly, while her green eyes sent in sparks. Trace just roll his eyes, "Kaden, wouldn't let you." was his response, before Elani tackled Trace down knocking the breath out of him.

They both struggled on the ground rolling over and over.
So it was a front, that Elani shown her a few hours ago.

"Get off of me witch." Trace hissed, not his character at all, as Elani landed a slap across of his right cheek.
They were both acting like total children.

Esmee closed her eyes annoyed,
first she was kidnapped and now this?
Where the heck is Kaden?
Why leave two idiots watching over her?

Cain...

She could barley picture him in her head.

Why didn't Diamond warn her of this?

Because she's a bitch that's why

Elani kicked Trace in his stomach, making him fall back on his back. He held his stomach with his arms, hissing in pain.

Elani stood up and dust herself off gracefully,
"If you just shut up then you wouldn't be in this much pain." She then left after a few minutes.

Esmee stared down at Trace.
Serves him right.

"Witch." he muttered, sitting back up rubbing his stomach. The bruise began to heal up and the pain is fading away.

"are you all right?"

Trace looked at Esmee surprised at her question.
"Why? What did you do-"
"I did nothing! I'm just wondering if you okay."

Esmee turned her face away, but it was obvious she was embarrassed to ask that question.

"I'm fine...Thanks for asking." Trace said uncomfortable, and at the moment the two of them were for once acting like friends...Distant friends.

Chapter 15: Couldn't bring myself

She would of thought that being kidnapped would be a lot more worse than this. They haven't torture her, sure they kept her tied up and bonded in a dark cold room at the end of a hall that leads to a dead in. Kaden made Trace stayed behind to keep a close eye on Esmee and at times Elani came in, sometimes peeking around the door entrance, only to see Esmee and Trace talking to each other like long lost friends.

One mistake through, Elani told Kaden that Trace had been flirting with Esmee and Kaden haven't take it well. He threw a fit that Esmee is a prisoner and captive and she will be treated as one, but when Trace throw the small fact of torturing in Kaden's face, he paled, and shuted his mouth leaving Elani gaped behind him.

"Elani don't like me." Esmee spoke, leaning on the slimy wall as Trace sit across of her on his knees looking at her questioningly.

"What do you mean She doesn't like you? She's like that to everyone through." Trace shrugged his shoulders, the strap from his black blazer almost slipped off his shoulder showing his well tone chest.

At times Esmee wished that Trace would dress RIGHT for once. What's wrong with a button up shirt with some jeans? Kaden is wearing some, so it must be alright in the demon realm. What makes Trace so special? Esmee sighed under her breathe. Coming all the way from the human world only to be kidnapped in the demon world.

"Really? She seem to like you."

Trace rolled his blue eyes at Esmee's suggestion.

"Stop playing around like that through, I hate her. I hate everything about her. Her voice, the way she speaks, the way she dresses and her entire personality. She has

78

nothing good to say to anyone and if someone dare to cross her on her bad hair day she totally flips out and went all crazy." Trace ranted, moving his hand side by side.

A small giggle left Esmee's lips at Trace being over dramatic because of Kaden's annoying sister Elani.

Elani...Elani Star...Elani Star Slade...
She was beautiful in a dark way.

A smile twisted on Trace's face at the recolonization of what is happening. He playfully slapped Esmee's arm. "Stop giggling at me. It's true! Try to be with that witch for 10 minutes!" Trace exclaimed, he stretched out his legs, brushing against Esmee's feet.

They both felt like a pair of normal teenagers at a slumber party without the danger of being kidnapped a possibility of being killed.

The color of her skin drained from her face at the thought and Trace caught it unlike anyone else that didn't really know her.

His voice softened-"He's not going to hurt you, you know."

Her eyes glazed at him, seeing that he looking dead at her now. His voice changed, not like him at all.

"What?"

"If he haven't torture you within the first two hours of your being kidnapped, then he's most likely not going to hurt you through this ordeal." Trace explained. Esmee's heart beats a little faster hearing this news. He wouldn't hurt her.

"What about you? Would you hurt me?" The question came off innocent and scare like, always asked by a child, and it seemed to fit for Esmee.

Trace shook his head after moments of thinking.

"No, I couldn't bring myself to hurt you." something in his voice once again changed, transformed into something else, as Trace inched himself closer to Esmee, who crawled backward a few inches the best she could away from him and his strange behavior.

He stopped when he's half way over her, before retreating back with a confused expression on his tired face. He glanced over Esmee's scared form before turning away, gathering back his sense and what had just happened.

It was stronger now, these strange feelings and normally Trace would easy fought them off like they did in the Human Realm.

'It's gaining strength, with each attack.' he figured.

"H-Hey are you okay?" Her voice broke through his inter-walls of his mind and he almost hissed at her to shut up, but stop himself once more. What's wrong with him?

"I'm fine. Sorry, I got carried away." Trace darkly said, before thrown himself back into his spot on the floor, faraway from any contact of human, demon or angel touches.

"Are you sure?"

"Yes, I'm fine. This is like the third time you asked me this and my answer is the same." Trace bit back the slid remark that is sure to come in due time. Why is he holding back? He should of release his full on rage on her completely. He's a demon.

80

It's his job to do so.

"Okay then."

No one talked for at least a minute. The silence almost suffocated her, until she broke it once more.

"Want to play the game 20 questions. Something to pass the time." Esmee suggested, and Trace raise up his eye brow at her strange.

"A human game?"

Esmee nodded her head- "Yes, but it's decent. We each asked a question to each other taking turns till we reached 20." She explained-
"Fine, you start Human" He phrase the last word in mocking way, but Esmee could tell he was just playing with her.

Same old Trace, had returned.

"What's your favorite color?"

"Green. Do you know Cain Heartwell?"

"Yeah, he's once my teacher. How you know him?"

"eh he's my cousin."

"Cousin!" Esmee gasped out surprised,
Trace nodded her head.

"Yeah, just adoptive cousin. He hates me. So when do you know your a halfy?" Trace asked, causal and Esmee realized that this game is going to get personal very sooner than she thought it was.

"eh just a few months ago." Esmee lied, trying to play it off that she didn't totally just found out a day ago.

"So your born a demon?" Curiosity caught up with her, and Trace stayed quiet for the longest.

"No, not really. You see Esmee, we all have a choice at the end to what we can become. Become an angel or demon. Many of us made mistakes, when we choose our paths our interests grew and changed. I first killed five years ago, when one of those idiots of a human corner Cain and I, threatening to stab us if we don't hand over the money."

The look on Trace's face was serous. They no longer playing the human childish game that humans grew interest in.

The way Trace explaining the demon crap was terrifying. He didn't show no other emotion than causal and with comfort, like this doesn't bother him at all of what he had done.

"What happened?" She whispered and a dark look passed over his face for a small second before going back to normal.

"When I killed him, Cain betrayed me. He hated what I become, but if I didn't kill the lowlife human he would of taken our life without hesitation. Cain disowned me, after he found out my secret...That I'm a demon...A creature of the night and murder of the dark. My interests began to grew and grew into the things you don't want to know and the human boy I once am is gone. I met Kaden next. Kaden didn't disowned me that my dearest cousin did because of whom I am. He accepted me..."

A sad look went over his face, a mere basic human emotion. Almost hard to detect on his face, was now shown. The betrayal and the kill had taken a toll on him and she just noticed the reason why he didn't seem to bothered at first is that of his once human defences mentally to keep people at bay. This teen in front of her is hurting for years and years of pain. The unknown pain that he hid for so long, and it's almost unbelievable that he told her this much.

"He must of did the same to you when he found out"

Esmee shook her head- "I didn't told him yet and now I'm afraid that if I will he will be his old self that you explained."

A harsh laugh escaped Trace's lips-"I'm glad that you didn't make the stupid mistake I did."

The air around them is lighter than before and they could feel the bond between them forming closer together very tight.

His heart beats heavier in his chest and his breathing became very hallow. Here's the second attack, he crunched his hand over his chest. He leaned forward clenching his teeth down, as a small hiss left his teeth.

Esmee barley stood up fast, before dropping back down worrying-
"Trace, are you okay? Your not aren't you!" Esmee gasped out worrying, she crawled towards Trace, whom waved at her to stay away.

"I-I'm fine-"

then Elani appeared at the door a look of disgust appeared on her face. Kaden appeared behind her. "What's happening?"

"It's the girl! She needs a bath! She somehow develop a poisonous scent..Must of got it from the Crimsion Lake. She absorbed most of there emotions, and this is why Trace and you are acting strange." Elani explained to Kaden, who ran pass her and half carried Trace out the room in lightning speed. "Take her a bath fast!"

A arm reached Esmee's jerking her forward roughly.
What's happening! She's so confuse, she could feel Elani hand gripped her arm very hard and the spot began to hurt.

"Oww it hurts." Esmee muttered, before being thrown in the room next to her somewhat cell.

"Disgusted creature." Elani splatting, and suddenly small water drops fell from the cracks of the castle ceiling. Her clothes were soaked again, as she fell to her knees due of the blinds.

A few tears mixed with the water on her face.
Is Trace alright?
Is he okay?

"You have one warning, halfy, stay away from Trace. If you stay away from him I'll make sure your worthless life is spared." Elani's voice entered Esmee's head, but still she remained emotionless on the floor, quietly sobbing to herself.

This wasn't her fault.

Trace reminded her of herself...So much of herself. He's afraid of rejection just like her.

Chapter 16: Diamond v.s Kaden

Diamond flew across the demon realm in high-speed, dodging the dark demon black crows on her way, she looked down and to her surprise the Crimson Lake was drained. Not single red drop left, not even the monster that haunts the lake is there hiding anymore.

There is a good chance that Esmee didn't make it in the demon world. The Crimson Monster is sort of like a gate keeper of the demon world. The people who traveled through the portal always appears above the lake in some form or another and like always the Crimson Monster will greet them with their fits of jealousy and hatred, only the strongest can get through.

The lake was drained, which surprised Diamond. Who had the power to do this? Certainly not Esmee, that is for sure. She just discovered her powers, too weak to even put on a good fight against anyone.

Diamond stretched her eyes to the beyond the dark gray clouds and the sudden sparks of lightning. The demon realm is very different from Heaven. There was a castle in the distance from the lake. The castle stood high on the rocks, looking like any human gothic castle.

What is the reason for Diamond to travel to the demon realm? Well to check up on Esmee of course.

Before Diamond could even fly a few more yards to the castle, a flash of lightning came close to hit her. She straggled backward just in time to dodge the second spark.

"Well, Well I was wondering what this strange aura belongs to, but sadly it's just you Diamond." said a very familiar dark voice in the gray of the clouds. Diamond focus her vision and hearing up in the sky from where she floated.

"Kaden, what are you doing here?" Diamond splatted out of her lips in disgust. There was a flow of silence that follow Diamond's somewhat command of question.
"heh I'm wondering the same to you. You don't belong to this world, you made my trip rather easy. I must thank you. I was planning to return for revenge." and with that said, a huge bolt of lightning struck down on to Diamond.

Her wings twitched wildly and a terrifying scream left her lips. Her eyes widened, as she felt thousand's of walts entered her angel like body suddenly, freezing up her human nerves. Her brain went hay wall* off the charts as she tried to gather her own mind, trying to counter this but there is no way to really counter lightning when it struck you.

A loud cranked of laughter left Kaden's lips as he finally revealed himself from the clouds above, gliding down to the bolt of lightning where it still strucking Diamond. Diamond crunched her teeth, biting back her own scream.
Make it stop, Make it stop! Her own nerves screamed, but it was ignore when Diamond doesn't want to give in.

"You know Diamond, demons here can easy control there climate without much interference, and you know what is better?" Kaden whispered, floating beside the huge bolt of lightning.

"I have Esmee."

The bolt of lightning disappeared, and Diamond body flew down. Her wings failed her for once and she's falling to her death.

Kaden watched Diamond fell without any lick of emotion. A grin appeared on his face as the feeling of Diamond's falling eyes stared into his own, shocked and in pain.

But suddenly a portal appeared under Diamond and she went right through, closing a few slow moments later.

Kaden didn't went after her. He just got rid of a problem, and she wasn't strong enough to survive a huge bolt of lightning.

The floor below her came too fast and she screamed on impact when her back hit the hallway's inside the portal. Her heart beat faster than normal and her muscles flinched whenever she tried to move and then the pain came once more. So she be still. The best way for her to numb the pain . She looked up at the ceiling weakly, she used the last of her power to summon a portal out of the blue to transfer her to safety.

That was skilled. She closed her eyes as the last wonders of Kaden entered her mind. He have Esmee. He kidnapped her, and there was nothing Diamond could do to save her either.

The feeling of helpless almost settle in her brain when a small pop can be heard in a small distance.

A man with short brown hair came out of the demon realm portal 2, his coat hugged his body, and his face looked sour for some reason. It's Cain!

Diamond flinched, trying to make any kind of movement to attract Cain's attention. The pain entered once more, and she screamed. Cain's attention was turned to her shocked, and surprised. He rushed over to her in an instant, a worry look on his face.

Chapter 17: The World Shattered

She lied...She didn't leave for her aunt's house for some fresh air! She actually went straight to the demon realm with no protection to look for some person..How can she be so damn reckless! What will she protect herself? She's just a lowly human barely with no special powers, except the sight.

Cain bit his lip, drawing blood, processing the information that Diamond is giving him at the last of her shallow breath before the darkness takes her away for a short amount of time.

"I was looking for Esmee, when Kaden came out of nowhere and attacked me. He can and other demons can easy control the climate...I wanted to see if Esmee is okay, even if I could be a little bossy. I wanted to give her something that could even protect herself within Kaden's domain...I made horrible mistakes...sending out a girl...human at that to take care of my job for me...I'm so stupid." Diamond whispered the last word, before she starts to close her eyes and the light from the halls went dim and dimer by the second.

Cain shook Diamond, "Are you okay?" That is all he could ever vocalize to the once bossy archangel, Diamond that he knew so well.

Diamond eyes opened and her vision was blurry just a bit. She nodded her head weakly.

88

"I-I'm a fast healer...but Esmee is not..You must save her. You have to." the disparate need in Diamond's voice had almost made Cain choose his own path already.

Cain let go of Diamond's shoulders, his hazel eyes in the shadows. His throat dried- Why should he go? She lied to him.

He somewhat have a feeling that Diamond is not telling him the ENTIRE story at all...She's leaving a huge piece out.

His heart tugged, remembering her note of farewell.

She's his former student...and his friend that they both shared common things.

He must try to save her.

"Where is she?" His voice was apathetic and Diamond found herself frown downheartedly at him.

"I-in the demon portal two.-"

Cain was about to move to the second demon gate to his right, before he was stopped by Diamond's weak voice.

"Kaden is too strong, reach in my pocket and get two scrolls. One for you and one for Esmee. Repeat the chant you grew accustom to. These are naturally, powerups in human terms."

Cain reached inside of Diamond's pocket, pulling out two blue scrolls, a feeling of guilt slammed into, and he looked down at Diamond's broken body with pity.

His face shown it.

"Go, I'll be fine..."

Then he was gone. Gone from the hallways, known as limbo.

Diamond rolled to her side weakly, closing her eyes, still feeling the pain traveling through her nerves. Oh lord finish me...

.~.

Just great, she is now fully transform back into her human self, which Trace barely gave her a glance. He ignored her since she had took her so called bath. The emotions from the Crimson Monster must of really caused the change in him, but now he's really different...Not himself anymore...Not the Trace she got to know a few hours ago.

"T-Trace?" She stumbled over her voice, as she rolled up in a ball in the corner of the dark cold room. The shadow at the door, didn't react as his name being called. She felt her insides torn, and she caught herself from thinking she still have the monster's emotions on her. She wanted Trace to talk to her...Be her friend...Was all he said is a lie? Demons lie, so it's understandable.

Her throat begins to itch as she coughed loudly, bright red liquid came out of her mouth almost making her scream in fright. What the hell is this! She's dying, she's sick! She only saw this on movies back home. How the patient always cough up blood and then hours later she die.

She must not scream, even if the thought of actually dying is coming to her...She must remain calm and strong...They were after her mother right? It seems...and they need her to find her...but wait..If they need her to look for her mom then would it be better

90

if she just die here, protecting her mother whereabouts? No...She don't want to die and she doesn't even want her mom to get hurt, even if she didn't see the woman most of her life.

Her human memories are fading slowly, now in the back of her head she could barely feel it. The feeling of hopelessness settled within her...She will die here in this awful room like many others that she didn't know about much.

A loud click can be heard through out the room and Trace stood beside as a bigger figure took it's place. 'Kaden'. He worn a vain smirk, and his voice was somewhat prideful.

"Guess, what little birdy come and fly into the cage." Kaden's voice radiated the cold room, but it was easy to tell he was talking to his buddy Trace.

Trace shook his head-"Who?"

"that witch of an angel, Diamond. I struck her with a bolt of lighting and she went falling."

at the end of the sentence, her eyes widened. His voice didn't betrayed any emotions that he's lying at all.

A new feeling of anger bubbled in her stomach and a growl left her lips angry. Diamond...Diamond had caused her so many problems, but she mean well in her strange way...Diamond being defeated, was a huge shock along the anger she felt.

Even through one side of her have a small crush on him, but he's hurting her friends and love ones now...First Cain and now Diamond? How many more will he hurt till

91

he stopped? A lot more, including her Mom.

An evil crackled left Trace's lips-"Finally you got that bitch."

and Esmee's world shattered, this wasn't the Trace she knew. The Trace she talked to moments before. Her friends are getting hurt and most likely killed...All because of her in some form..Why...Why did god hate her so much?

'because your half demon, that's why' a dark voice answered her in her head brutally.

Chapter 18: We is a big word

Ivory Lock, amazing woman of her age stood in front of her bedroom window watching the already dark clouds turned even darker. The sight before her was disgust her to the core of her very being, but what could she do. Half of her powers are well gone, she is still considered as a teen here in the demon realm even through she's twice matured than her father, she's a female and therefore must marry to gain the thrown of the demon realm, and her father trapped her here, than the human world...The human world of where she belonged..Where she should be in now instead of staying in this prison with no hopes of escaping...No she spend 12 years here, it was time to leave...

So how to get rid of Tom? No...The reason why she stayed so long here is that if her father found out about her daughter or husband, he would kill them, seeing their race. Even if her daughter is half demon. Human beings valued flesh and blood, but not so much as demons.

Normal demons would turn on you in an instant if you off your guard.

So this means she have to get rid of both Tom and her father..

Kill them in their sleep? No, demons have heighten senses in the demon realm...They could easy sense her within the room.

Rebellion? Maybe that would work...She easy gather a few demons, creatures and half demons to rebel against her father and Tom. She could gathered the humans that they slaved from the plane!

The door to her room cracked opened, as the voices of her father and her 'dearest' Tom could be heard.

"Impossible, the Crimson Monster is defeated?" Her father voice was steady and stern, didn't believe a word that Tom had told. Her father had faced the so called Crimson Monster, and only barely escaped with his life before he was crowned, of the demon realm and the monster have to listen to him.

"I'm afraid so, sir. I flew across of the Crimson Lake, and saw every drain of red liquid, gone. The only thing there is the Crimson Castle, where Elani Star is living upon." Tom explained, just as his dark eyes reached Ivory. He placed a false smile upon his face.

"Hello, Ivory." Grabbing her soft hand, pressing his lips on the front kissing it, french style. Ivory held her negative emotions back just in time, as a fake smile of her own reappeared on her tired face.

"Hello, my dearest Tom." The sentence was laced with sarcastic, that Ivory found it surprising that her father and Tom didn't even detect.

Her father looked troubled, before he fixed his gaze to her.

He nodded his head in approval, seeing her demon wings are popped out from her back, her demon form.

"Okay, if Tom is saying is true, we must check this out fast as we could."

"W-We?"

"Yes we, this will be both of you first assignment." Her father glared, and suddenly Ivory decided that the word 'We' its just too big for her to understand in demon terms.

Chapter 19: The Power in His Hands

Her wings twitched in place, she couldn't flattered them out of her back fully anymore. She is truly in her human state of transformation...Weak..Now she's totally weak and helpless, unable to do anything, trapped in a demon prison till her utmost death.

Her powers failing each time she closed her eyes and tried to used them, due of her human handicapped within the demon world. Her eyes opened within a few minutes as she struggled to sit up straight against the gruesome sticky walls beside her, but then her back started to hurt and she stopped her movement.

The friend she found in Trace was no more. He was just like her...afraid...What is he exactly afraid of?

His stoned gaze turned to her. He worn a familiar emotion that she have plenty of experience with. Anger...and then a fade emotion even called cruelty. A real demon.

"What are you looking at with that gaze, weakling?" He said this cold and it had hurt her emotionally.

"Nothing" Esmee whispered, glancing away.

He's totally different from the last time they have met in the hospital. He was nicer there than here, and he changed.

Her joints were sore from earlier and her vision became a little blurry, losing her focus for once.

Soft and graceful rhythm of footsteps reached her hearing, but Trace still stand still by the doorway, not moving a inch.

Then the footsteps stopped, and Esmee looked up to it's owner, not surprise to see Elani, in a different dress than before.

Elani looked at both her and Trace with an unreadable face, before it was once again masked.

"Charles de Chaos and Tom de Slade is arriving soon for Crimson expection." Elani snarled the first name with such hatred, that it seemed almost impossible to have felt and do ever, but considering she's a full demon it's normal.

Elani still doesn't look anything related to Kaden, much less his own sister.

Charles de Chaos...Sounds familiar to her, like she suppose to know this person and it's name.

Tom de Slade...Can it be? Kaden's and Elani's father? Esmee throat dry once more and her heart beat raced a small bit.

"So?" Trace said cold, from the side of the door.

Elani rolled her dark eyes at his stupidly.

"Charles de Chaos RULES the Demon Realm within the following week till his daughter and her newly wed husband, Tom de SLADE rules." Elani snarled at him which he just glared at her with cold dark eyes of his own.

Diamond...The heard of her own defeat was still flesh in her mind. Is she hurt? Badly? From what Kaden talking arrogantly about, she is.

'I want to go home'

but where is home? Her human mind couldn't even remember.

Another set of footsteps came in place, and stopped beside of Elani.

"Here's the plan, get ready, we are setting a ransom to Charles de Chaos for his granddaughter." Came Kaden's voice, and then he appeared.

"Granddaughter!"

.~.

He gripped the scrolls in his hands tight, his knuckled bruised, remembering Diamond weak voice and bruise up body, he bit his lip down for the second time, causing it to bleed once more, in frusation.

When he went through the portal 2 of the demon realm everything went sudden black, he couldn't see anything, and then he was falling downward to a dark cold PIT of darkness. A sheik left his pale thin lips, at the sudden surprise.

He placed Esmee's scroll in his pocket, leaving his out. He piled it open desperately, he wasn't afraid of falling, but he is afraid of breaking his own bones.

The scroll actually swung opened, floating in front of him, going down at a steady pace. Humans aren't meant for flying... He could feel the energy of the scroll by him. Strange chiense letters was written in the scroll, glowing bright blue. Each letter disappeared right after another, making Cain confused.

He felt a small spark on his figure tips and on his upper back, as two huge white angel like wings pop out of his shoulders, stinging him a little bit. He bit back the scream, looking down at his hands next. The sparkles of the letter combined together, revealing a sword. A sliver long blade sword, for combat and when he touched the said weapon he felt he was in control for once, but the sword wasn't only a sword. The top of the sword opened like a lid, revealing a huge black shotgun.

A grin reached his lips. He have close distance and long distance weapon packed in one, one strong weapon that only he himself could control.

His wings flapped opened widely in the black sky and with each stroke he floated in the air and into safety of the drop.

He closed his eyes, feeling the supernatural power being absorbed through his skin and mixed in his human blood.

He have the power now.

The power to end this fuel between demons and humans once and for all. He will teach them the lesson that humans are the supior race.

He have the power in his hands.

"but what about Esmee?" a little voice in his head asked, weakly.

Chapter 20: Cain v.s Elani

He felt the power going through the veins in his blood system. Is this what it felt like to finally be strong? Finally able to fight back without much of a struggle from anyone? Knowing that this power could end the fuel? He nearly felt the excitement coming through him, when the sky above him suddenly clear up, showing him some light.

Beneath him, was a dry up lake or pond. Lifeless without anything to live upon, but the water that should filled this lake or pond up is red...Red liquid...Blood. His face twisted in disgust, when the stench of the dry and old blood reached his nose.

Disgusted...A few screams can be heard from below and this is a curse. They were nothing more than ghosts without their shell.

A wave of compassion shot through his mind like a flying bullet watching the shadows on the ground gathered up and cry together in pain of their past. Some of them stopped a few seconds before crying once more.

Cain felt himself lower towards them and then stopped, seeing their is exactly nothing he could ever do. He could only save the living, not the dead. A painful emotion reached his face when debating on what to do next.

"Help..." His mind went a little fuzzy, before he flapped his white wings to go sideways. Flying crooked, like a hurt bird he was away from the dry up lake. He looked up, seeing a black castle in a distance. Something telling him, that this was it. He held his sword tighter than normal, as fear rushed into his body.

Why should he be afraid of? Dying? No, she can't be afraid of that

Their was lightning flashing above him, when he decided to fly lower to aviod a higher chance to be struck like Diamond.

He wasn't that stupid.

He's went to college for god sakes and took Physics.

The tallest object always have a higher chance to be struck down.

He's human with angel powers. Human body is made up of almost 80 percent of water. Lightning effects water, so it would be dire if it struck him ever so.

The castle is getting close and closer to his view,when the clouds begins to dark even darker.

He faked his sword in front of him when he saw a hallow shadow of a person flying in the air infront of him suddenly.

It was shaped in a form of a girl from the looks of it. She held a huge wooden staffed in her hands, that could deal great damage if used correctly.

Cain didn't blinked back one bit, as he stopped flying right in front of her. Her bat like wings stretched somewhat wider than his own. Her raven hair was wild and her eyes narrowed at the site of him, before she coldly laughed.

"You? A human with wings, I see everything now." She laughed, before lowering her staff not seeing him as a real threat.

She was a demon and Cain have a natural boiling anger for her at it is.

"I give you another chance, seeing I'm in a hurry. If you just leave now, I wouldn't have to kill you." She offered, before Cain's the top of his sword flipped opened, revealing the top of a shotgun. He fired it, and she barely blocked it with her staff, pushing her backward a small bit from the impact. Her eyes narrowed once more harder at this fact.

"I see your not like all the others..." She lopsided smile, just as Cain is getting ready to fire another shot, that he now aimed to kill. He have no mercy within his hazel eyes.

The woman took a few more minutes to look him over before she finally spoke once more.

"a Supernatural Official right? I wonder why your here? Maybe it have something to deal with that brat of a girl?"

The top of Cain's sword closed, when the woman spoke once more. She was doing all the talking like always.

"I'm Elani Star, the last name you will be hearing before joining the afterlife." She grinned, her staff grown two inches taller.

Cain placed his sword right in front of him, with a fierce look of determination on his face. She said the brat of a girl, meaning Esmee...She's here..and to save her he have to go through this witch first.

"Cain Heartwell, last name before you go to eternal hell." and with that they both crashed their weapons against eachother with such force that they almost knocked eachother back.

The blade of the sword didn't slice the wooden weapon, meaning the demon's weapon is more than it looks.

They clashes their weapons once more each with the will to kill another. Cain shifted his weapon sideways, blocking her staff in the progress, pushing it away from her chest with such ease. He aimed a kick to her stomach, knocking the breathe right out of her lungs, flying backward.

Her wings flapped back and forth stopping her movement.

She hissed at the thought of being evenly match with a human.

"DIE!" She screeched, swinging her staff, a huge gust of wind escaped the staff flying towards Cain, who held his sword in a defensive position. His wings flapped forward, as the wind slammed into him pretty hard. He crunched his teeth, feeling his blood turning cold of this impact. His eyes closed due of his human reflexes, and when he finally got it opened again Elani's fist connected to Cain's face, making him lose his balance and fall downward.

He thrust his sword upward, slashing her own wing and she too fell downward into the black abyss of the location below them.

Cain flapped his wings back and forth and he creased the speed of his landing while Elani flapped her wings like a weaken bird, the blood flew upward from the wound he gave her.

Then their bodies both hit the ground and his heart stop beating automatically. His muscles stopped working and his nerves went hay wire. His hazel eyes widened, feeling the pain in his chest over come him and the slowing heart beat of his own heart.

No... He mustn't die like this! He refuse. He refuse. But their was nothing he could even do to save himself like this. His hazel eyes watered for the first time since his cry when his ex girlfriend Jen left.

He doesn't want to die like this.

A picture of Esmee flashed in his head and then a image of Diamond. He broken his word and with the last of his heart beat he closed his eyes, a few of his tear drops washed onto the dented up ground.

Elani couldn't move. She just couldn't. Her heartbeat his alive and well but her nerves are gone. Just gone, and she couldn't move from her position. She looked sideways and saw Cain's lifeless pale body, and a victory grin placed on her face before she too went into eternal sleep.

A small light glow above Cain's chest, slowly going within him within a few seconds the moment his breathing stop. His mind is troubled, in his final moments. The light of his own soul. The light of his own soul quickly transformed into a human figure, most likely himself in his ghost form.

He looked down at his shell with an unknown emotion. He couldn't do anything now he have failed. A tugged pulled within his chest. Why must it have to end like this?

A transparent tear fell from his eyes. He couldn't held it back anymore.

Why is he here now? He read from the scrolls that once a person dies it souls traveled back to the limbo to awaits judgement...unless the ghost stills hanging onto something.

He looked at the castle.

Right..Esmee.

He couldn't save her and then he looked at Elani. A rush of unexpected anger went through him as he gild to her lifeless body.

It was all her fault!

She killed him.

It was all her fault that he couldn't save Esmee.

He went to kick her, but his leg went right through her.

"Shit" He cursed, before feeling a pull to his body. He let himself being pulled and then suddenly it was like his body is calling for him. Because now, he was back into his body once more. Because now he could live and breathe once again.

Chapter 21: Through Your Eyes

The scroll that Diamond gave her in the past hours had finally slipped out of her pocket wet and torn and by Kaden's feet when he went to grab her. He looked down at the scroll which read in Chinese-'Family Scroll and the Family Rulers of the Demon Realm.'

Interesting...He bent over and picked up the scroll the thin paper in his hands felt so weak that even if one tiny pull would destroy it. He glanced at Esmee who stared at him with those horrible blue human eyes of hers. The human eyes that he would like to wip right out of her eye sockets and shoved them down her throat, but he knew how to keep himself in check now.

He piled the scroll opened and a strange handwriting came in view...The letters was different from his abcs that he learned back in the day in the human world and this world. What is this language? It was angel like with too many markings and he growled to himself seeing that could be the secret of this girl family line. He just couldn't read it!

Esmee eyes widened fear, shot through her like a bullet. She couldn't move an inch. Her human blood froze within her and all she could ever do is watched helplessly as Kaden's eyes searched and think of away to read it.

"Kaden, what's the hold up?" Trace's voice echoed through the room with a little ring, his black-reddish eyes snapped to Trace. "Go look for Elani. It seems it would take a little longer here." He stated, getting back to the scroll. The footsteps echoed through out the castle halls, as Trace aura disappeared beyond the walls within a few minutes. He's gone, but it was obvious he would be back.

How to read the scroll..How to read it..

His eyes shifted to Esmee who trembled under his stare.

Can it be?

Yes it must be it! She's the key like always..

"You come here." He commanded, his hand reached her pale skin on her arm, grabbing her was easy, too easy. He pulled her close to him-the beat of her heart raced full speed.

"Read it." He pushed the scroll within her arms and her eyes scan the scroll automatically. The language that the scroll is written in is indeed Chinese. A language that she herself could not understand. What is Diamond thinking when handing her the scrolls of another language than her own?

Snow
The true heir of the demon realm will have to prove him or herself.
A key to the heart is the important key, a color of gold is to be unlock. The secrets will unraveled of a snowy night.
A mysterious secret will be reveal.

The words came out of her lips automatically, and she was surprised that she could read it. Her blood within her bubbling sightly, must be a demon thing...She decided somewhat. Kaden eyes narrowed and something triggered inside of him at the word 'snow' the words that Esmee read pondered in his mind.

Key...True heir...He then grabbed the scroll just as Esmee opened her mouth to speak. "Why do you want to rule the demon realm?"

He slapped her out of reflexes, which was pretty bad. She somewhat flew backward from the inhuman force and a whimper left her lips when she landed. She tried to sit up but fall right back on her side, in pain.

Her eyes dimming from any sign of real hope, bruised and wounded she just lied there...There in the darkness of the room and hearing the heavy angry breathing of Kaden.

Her cheek stinging from the slap he didn't hesitated to give her.

The realization of what he had just did finally shook Kaden as another emotion is shown on his face before it was covered with a mask.

"You don't need to know why." He hissed out through his fang like teeth, but it was easy to tell that he's hiding something.

"Get up, it's time to go."

Esmee didn't move. She just couldn't. Her spirit broken in shards.

Heavy footsteps came closer to her form before Kaden kneed down by her side checking.

Her eyes flickered to him out of impulse, her eyes pleading dimming, just dimming from anything else.

"Can't move or walk? Humans are such a waste." He muttered, picking her up and throwing her around his shoulder. Her body went limp, just behind her and couldn't bring herself to frown.

He stood up and walked out the door and to the outside as the flesh air reached her back. A tiny chill went down, as she looked over the horizon.

Her heart raced even more as Kaden actually drop her down on her back. Still couldn't move, she just stayed there, saving the rest of her strength just staring up at the dark night stars above. Her eyes watered, as a certain memory of a dark hair boy, Diamond and her flying up passing the moon and stars in the night sky.

A few tears escaped her eye lids, looking to her side as Kaden walked to the side of the roof top.

'I want to help you' her throat dried. I want to see through your eyes on why your doing this.

There it is. The smallest piece of hope and faith is actually still there. Then she scoffed to herself, of course it was still there. She's still half a human. Human always have faith and hope that almost couldn't be destroyed.

Chapter 22: Look Within Yourself

Cain barely have anytime to move up some more before he saw a figure of another demon.

'They're like cockroaches.' He thought disgusted, as he place his sword in front of him very weakly than before with not much strength. He knew this, but God gave him another chance to live and he's not going to waste it again this time. Elani, stayed emotionless a few feet away from him and he didn't really mind that she's still breathing. She's knocked out, that's whats counts at this moment.

The demon figure glided through the sky and now downwards, not flapping his wings much and a slight pull camethrough his heart that he almost hissed out in pain. The battle against Elani and him had taken their toll.

The demon landed on his feet, his wings went back into his midback, and Cain could see his smug expression.

"Cain, my long dear cousin. How are you these fine night?"

Cain flinched, he lower his sword a bit just as mix feelings entered his mind and soul. The demon before him was indeed his cousin...His cousin that he had long been betrayed because of his race and culture. The cousin he had witness murder a few people in the past. The cousin that is cursed with a life of hell and sorrow. He felt a small sparkles of regret and remorse, but still he kept his face emotionless.

He came in the light of the moon and he glanced down at Elani on the ground, he kicked her body a small bit to see if she's awake. But she didn't move, but he did see her chest raise and down taking in huge amount of air.

"I see you place dear old Elani in her place." He muttered, his blue eyes locked on Cain's hazel eyes just as the top of his sword flipped open revealing his dear old gun.

Trace raise his arms in front of him surrendering, which was strange.

"Woah! I'm not here to fight, calm down." Trace defended, seeing Cain's harden expression.

"Then what are you here?" Cain snarled out through his teeth, he haven't forgotten that they had tortured him.

Trace pointed at Elani's fallen form.

"for her and I have something I have to tell you. But first...I can see you actually don't have any strength for a long battle. So place down your sword slash gun." Trace said, pointed his figure then upward, just as a huge gust of wind came downward, slamming into Cain's arm that held his weapon.

A scream left his lips, as his weapon slipped through his figures and hit the ground

THEN slid down the location.

"Thats better."

Cain held his arm close to his body, looking at his weapon trying to see on how he could reach his weapon.

"Lord, you still want to fight me? I just here for a talk. I disarmed you, because I know your nature Cain. Remember that faithful day? Now be still and listen." Trace snorted, and Cain felt his blood ran cold and his feet stuck to the ground below him. He couldn't move. He was scared. Fear, frozen his body. Dammit!

"Now I got your full attention. I'm here to talk to you about the brat of a girl you're on a rescue mission on." He said, circling Cain slowly.

"I'm not here for some girl."

Trace scoffed-"Don't lie. I know you normally don't stroll in the demon realm for nothing, due of your hatred."

Cain kept silent.

It was true. If it wasn't the fact that Esmee is held prisoner, he wouldn't come this far.

"I'm surprise, I admit Cain. I never saw you go this far for anyone except, that girl Jen-"

"Don't talk about her!" Cain hissed and Trace blinked. He still have the soft spot to his ex girlfriend?

"but Heartwell, I do. You see it seems that you are using the brat as a replacement for your ex." Trace voice was laced with some other emotion.

Cain blood boil with anger at his mere suggestion.

Sure, Esmee watched after him when he's hurt and he looked after her when she's hurt it doesn't mean the way Trace is implying. Friends save Friends right?

"I spend alot of time with her lately and she told me something interesting, and I see something interesting within her eyes."

His footsteps stopped right behind Cain.

"You know that human's memories seemed to fade at some point in the demon world? She tried her best to remember you."

"She wants to be saved. She wanted you to save her...but at the last moment her will flickered like a flame on a 's gone. And it's your fault. You didn't save her and now she's gone." Trace grinned, and just then Cain moved his foot forward trying to overcome his fear of something. He was pissed, along with guilt. He found himself believing Trace.

"What do you mean she's gone? Dead?" Cain asked, sadness and anger laced his tone. If she's dead he will make Trace pay. He will make the bastard who killed her pay.

"Oh hells no. She's not gone gone. But Cain, you need to look deep down within yourself. What do you exactly feel about her? Her life is depending on your feelings." Trace told him, walking beside Elani, picking Elani upside ways. His wings pop out of his back and flapped open.

He glanced at Cain again-"ask yourself what will you do when you find out that your little Esmee, is not the girl you use to know."

and then Trace flew upward in the dark sky and Cain find himself moving once more. He fell to his knees looking down on the ground.

His breathing turned heavy, and his eyes widen. What does Trace mean about Esmee is not who she use to be?

He felt his soul shook and he looked at the castle in the distance that Trace flew off with Elani. A small blue reddish light appeared on the top, and the words-'Help me' ran through his brain in Esmee's voice.

She needs help.

Time wasn't on his side.

Chapter 23: Gone to the Deepest Part

*Your weak...Your always so weak. Why do you keep allowing this? Why do you keep on allowing yourself being abuse physically and mentally, when you have so much power following through your veins. You could easy crush this fool. Why hold yourself back? They hurt you far too much. Let me control you. Let me handle this. Just sit back and watch. I handle this work, human...*Esmee blinked, the tears away just as the voice voiced her opinion in her head rather snug. No...No she mustn't think thoughts about that...nor let her demon side take control...She's a good girl. She's human. She wasn't meant to be taken over...

but you are...You just didn't know it until now...

Then the two of her black bat like wings pop out from her back.

What are you waiting for? Some guy Cain to rescue you? Your not a maiden in

distress. You have power. Stronger than any human, if you lend me your body I will

granted your happiness.. Kaden looked at Esmee, with wonder. How can she regain

her powers so much easy in a short amount of time? She's a half demon and half

human, she wouldn't be able to heal this much at this speed.

A dark purple aura surrounded her small form, as her stomach inched upward in the

air, half of her body glued to the ground below. Her blue eyes rolled to the back of her

head only to be replaced by a deepish dark black pair of eyes. Her human like smile

turned lopsided, dark.

Her hair turned darker...a dark shade of brown almost black.

Let me have your body for a moment, Lock and I will make the pain go away...I

promise... She wanted the pain. The fight, everything to go away. She fought so much

and in a short time in her life. Trying to reach a parent that disappeared when you

were at least five, learning that your mom. Your own mother is held kidnapped for a

decade with her knowledge.

The pain of her family splitting apart when the plane is nowhere located on the

computer.

The pain that her ex step mother caused...

What is life to her? Life is meaningless and useless. A waste of existence. A part of

her doesn't want this kind of life anymore...but the other part..The human

side...wanted her life like this. Because the past struggles made her who she was now.

He's not coming...Let me save you. Your life is very dear to me, Esmee... A parasite...The mother's blood within her is like a parasite feeding on her anger, pain and hatred. Waiting for the right moment to attack...The moment where her true weakness is revealed.

She felt herself slipping away...Slipping away through the darkness of the Earth that her human self once roamed upon.

*What? You want to help that poor excuse of a demon? He isn't worth your pity...He will never become your friend. Not after what he just did. I wouldn't allow it!*No friends...Nothing to keep her going one bit...But she did have someone..She knew it! But her humanself could not remember much.

She could hear her demon side laughed within her mind loudly. Yes victory, is within reach. The battle between Esmee's human will against the demon's will had begun moments no hours ago.

Her mind blanked as the emotion of hopeless slammed within her. She's useless. She couldn't do anything right. With one last tear, she lost herself and the person she's is now is nothing more than a demon vessel.

"I finally meet you...face to face.." Esmee's voice changed, it had deepened. She stood up from the ground with such ease. Her eyes connected with Kaden's filled with such evil.

"She's not here to save you this time."

Claws, appeared out of Kaden's knuckles.

A small thin sword appeared in Esmee's hand from the dusk in the night sky.

Bloodlust thrust filled the air above.

"Payback is so sweet." and so they both charge towards eachother, only one thing on their mind. One of them going to live and another have to die.

Their wings pop back within their bodies. They don't need them to this fight at all.

Esmee is gone. Gone into the deepest part of her inner mind, leaving her demon self behind in control.

Chapter 24: To Wake Up

The two beings fought and despite her early attraction to the demon, she does not care much anymore. She does not harbor any of her former human emotions. She is like a whole new person or creature. Sword clashes with blades, and the impact of them both together send the two backward a small bit as bright blue sparks flew everywhere's. Esmee grip on the hilt of her sword is going strong and a look of frusation appeared on her demoniac face.

"I admit, your strong than most." She snarled, but strangely Kaden remained silent, swing up his steel claws and then down with little than no force. Something wasn't right here and her human senses would of told her so, but she was no more at this point. Esmee easy blocked the attack, pushing back his claws effortless.

He barely fought her off keeping the same old emotions, cold and blank on his face while doing so. She hated the sight of these emotions...

The tip of Esmee's blade light up with blue sparks, just tiny sparks that waved off power. Power that her human self do not have.

Esmee found herself hating this being in front of her that is blocking her own attacks and then barely attacking her unlike the first swing.

"Show something else!"

But before she could actually strike him again something slammed into her back like a speeding bullet, knocking the breathe right out of her demon lungs.

The scent of blood, her blood filled the area and a hissed left her lips, landing down to her knees. The wings on her back folded up unwilling, feeling the flowing of her blood coming down of her back.

She touched her back, feeling for any sign of injury, only to find just one. Major, one on the middle of her back. It was deep, and she wonder who had snuck up behind her to deliver the blow. Cannot be Kaden, seeing he's right in front of her...but...

"I see your being a bad, girl while I'm gone." The familiar voice of Trace filled the air, and she snapped her head in his direction to see the viewing.

Trace floated to his feet, his wings folded to his back and within his arms the body of Elani can be seen, but when he reached the ground he threw her on the sidelines without much care.

"Where have you been?" snapped Kaden, turning his attention to Trace, his mistake as Esmee half limped towards Kaden her sword right in front of her body in a pity and desperate last strike to do some damage, only to be stop when Kaden slapped her blade with his claws without much interference about anything. The sword slid out of Esmee's fingers tips and landed on the ground making a huge noise.

The feeling of his claw pressed against her throat slightly only making a small cut. Bright red liquid flow downward.

"Your lucky I'm holding you ransom. Otherwise, I would of done finish you off." He hissed, and then in a second his claws is gone, and he glided a few spaces away.

Her red eyes widened and suddenly she begin to cough up blood, but yet she didn't felt any fear.
She turned to him sharply- "Kill me! Finish the job!"
But her hatred cries were ignore. Rage filled her instantly.

⁓

It was dark that is all she can see and tell. Her feet reached nothing down below and it was like she's just floating around with much thought. She tried to open her eyes wider, but she could only see nothing. A sigh left her thin bruised lips, just as a wind of voices floats all around her now.

Where is she? She does not know.
A pounding feeling met her back when she heard herself saying the words she would never have said in a life time.
"Kill me!"

Was that really her?
No...No...

She is sleeping...Somewhat.
No dreams, but she could hear anyone.
She just needs to wake up, but how?

No one will not come and save her from this problem she got herself into. Cain wasn't here to save the day.

Then a surprising realization hit her.

She remembered everything!

She left Cain behind in search of her mother and only to be kidnapped by Kaden and Trace. Her home is within the human world...

She has people to go back to.

Yeah that's right she needs to wake up, but once again how?

~.~

"How long do we have to wait?" Trace questioned, watching Esmee form curl up in a tiny painful ball on the ground.

"Not long," Replied Kaden, only to be shut up when a small blue light enclosed Esmee form blinding the two of them, due of their extra sense of sight.

A painful scream left her lips and slowly drowning out by her own deep and hallow breathing. Her eyes transform back to her normal color.

Her weapon disappeared in a sparkle of blue dusk in the night's sky.

She's human once again.

She is now awake.

Chapter 25: Hope is all Humans Have

A tiny spark of hope rushed in her head with the mix of fierce determination she soon to be delvoping within her soul. No one was coming to save her, it's all on her. She will save and rescue her mother and no one will stop her.

Not like this. She had no idea where this new found determination and hope came from, maybe it was all that time being torture that this came from. She doesn't want to give up in to these losers.

She stood up but almost fell down to her knees, due of the extrusion and physical pain. Relief, went through the demons features. The look on Trace's face was at first soft before transforming back in that ugly grin or smirk, that he always worn to cover up his regular emotions.

A bang of thunder echoed through out the sky and then the castle. The tensions began to mix with something else. Something else more frightful, and blueish lightning flashed through the dark grey clouds.

Kaden placed his arms in front of his head, protecting himself for some unknown reason.

"Brace yourselves!" He called out to Trace and he didn't need to be told the second time, when he flew to Elani's side, leaving Esmee alone and confused.

Brace herself for what? Another sound of thunder roared through the air more violently and the vibrations shook the castle roof as three features came in view in the sky, flying downward to them. From a distance, they can easy be tell that they hold true power. Power...That word send shivers down her nervous system, freezing her in place and her nerves went wild, but it wasn't enough to drive out her pervious emotions. She's scared, sure. Her human self is reacting natural to such power.

They came closer in a steady beat and speed, and Trace kicked Elani's body without much thought at the moment. "Wake up, they're almost here." Trace hissed, kicking her side once more and once again found no movement. She's still comatose.

"Leave her be, we handle this by ourselves. Same plan." Order Kaden, harshly-

"and besides, there is no way we can lose this battle." He grinned smog like and when his words filled the air a sudden realization drawn to her. The scent of death is laced in the air.

Trace turned to Esmee angry, giving up waking Elani and following Kaden's advice.

"You just hold still and restrained anymore movement. With each movement your wound will grow." He mocked at her human weakness. Esmee narrowed her eyes at him, just as the three figures feet touched the roof top.

'I don't want to fight like this.' but of course she would just have to. Everything doesn't always go as planned.

"Kaden." The man in the far left stiffly said, very cold.

"Father." Kaden repeated in the same tone of voice without any more emotion.

True Demons.

The man on the far right look mad, peeking over the edge of the castle of the roof only seeing small droplets of red down below.
The lake was nomore. This is proof to him.

His dark eyes switched to the two girls on the floor most likely helpless, who is either in pain or in a state of comatose.

'Human' his senses told him and he could barely resisted the urge to throw himself on the poor girl and tear her lim to lim. She didn't show any sign that a human would shown in this kind of situation and he ponder if she really is human at all.

Blood...

Human blood.

She's wounded.

"What the hell happened here?" He demanded.

The woman in the middle flinched annoying.

When her gaze reached Esmee's her face paled.

A huge pull on Esmee's heart told her who this woman truly is.

"M-Mom?" The one word left her lips that surely made anyone tremble out crying at this moment, but Ivory held back that kind of emotion the best she could.

The woman just stood there shock.

"This is where the party begins."

Tom slid his hand in front of Charles just as both Kaden and Trace ran pass Esmee and towards the group of other demons.

"Let me handle this."

and then there was huge parks of yellow and then a painful scream can be heard as the woman in the middle flew over the edge of the castle falling...

"MOM!"

Esmee's world seemed to shattered once more and the pain settled at the pit of her stomach. It's happening over and over again. Why couldn't God leave her be and torture someone else for once?

Chapter 26: Please Save Her!

Why does it always have to be like this? She had just met her and just like this God had taken her away.

Esmee arms begin to twitch and for the first time in along time, raw anger flow down her. How many times have she have to witness for all this to stop?

She is pissed off, beyond that it seems to anyone near her.

A look of shock went on Trace's face-he wasn't suppose to attack the woman! Tom sword came out of the otherside of Charles stomach, blood rushing down the blade.

The metal claws were within a few inches to Charles neck and Trace took a huge leap over the edge, flapping his wings downward trying to catch up to Ivory to save her from her approaching death.

Charles looked up to his right hand man with a look of pure betrayal asking him why. Why, had he turned on him like this?

Tom twisted his sword within Charles stomach just as Kaden slice one cut on his neck.

"With you out of the way, it's easy to take over the demon world now. Without you, I can easy take over your daughter." hissed Tom, his hand tightens on the thin blade of the sword.

The pain lunched within Charles stomach, but he was nowhere near dying yet. He's powerful, it would take more than this to take down the ruler of the demon world.

Grandpa...

An unknown emotion ran in Esmee's mind. Even through, she didn't meet this man and she only heard bad things about him, but it doesn't take away the fact that he is family.

"Do you enjoy it?" Esmee voice was harsh and cold, standing up more straight now. Her eyes darkened with raw emotion, the pain in her joints kept her in reality.

Kaden, Tom and Charles eyes were on her this time. Tom and Charles surprised that this lowly human is voicing her opinion and talking to them. Kaden faced blank, eyes narrow telling her to shut the hell up and behave like a good little human girl.

"Do you enjoy tearing every single thing I ever care about! Her eyes were glassy, and a wave of demon aura escaped her body, surprising the two man.

She took a few steps forward, the roof crumbled with each step she took and she's glad that this rooftop is stronger than most.

"Pull that sword out of his body, and hope that my mother is alive and well. Before I break that sword for you." Her voice was deadly, and then suddenly the metal claws was away from Charles, and flying towards her.

Esmee kept her ground not even blinking and suddenly, her hand flew up meeting

Kaden's arm, ducking her head under his claws, she pushed him backward, causing him to almost lose his balance.

"Fool, do not insult my power when I'm angry." Her iron gaze went back to Tom, who twisted his sword deeper in Charles stomach. Charles placed two of his hands on Tom's sword, trying not be affected by Esmee's speech-'Mother'

"Slade, you choose the wrong demon to turn against." and with that Tom blade, break in half without much effort at all, surprising him completely, and then a huge fist went through Tom's stomach making him loose his breathing. He staggered backward in pain at the force of the impact.

Charles gaze turned to Esmee and his outlook changed. He then come to realize that she is a half demon and half human...Outsider of the two culture and race.

Rush of anger, went through him hotly. This human girl is the mistake of his daughter, and the disgraced of his royal blood line.

A huge gust of wind blow over them all, as Ivory flew up by herself with her wings spread out wildly, as Trace flew above her cutting her off easy.

Ivory hissed at him, before he tackled her to the rooftop, smashing her body to the roof. She then kicked him off, between his legs and he too backway in pain and hurt.

"Ivory, how could you..." Esmee grandpa whispered angry, under his breathe.

Esmee took a few steps towards her mother her own anger is fading, with each step her heart raced. This is her mom...

Emotions ran through her-

Happiness, anger, sadness, relief...

"Mom?"

Ivory smiled softly at her opening her arms wide inviting her to hug her and of course Esmee ran towards her and hugged her tight. Sobs, left her lips.

"M-Mom, I thought you were dead." She cried, as Ivory hands rubbed her head softly like a baby being put to sleep.

"Shhh, no need to cry. I'm here and alive." She whispered in her ear, only to be cut off by Charles angry aura.

"Ivory, how could you disgrace the line like this?" He roar, obvious of the scene he placing.

Ivory kissed Esmee on her forehead, letting her go before facing her father with new found courage.

"Father, I didn't disgrace the bloodline. I hate my title and blood here and I don't know if I hate you so much to kill you now for what you did. You can't stop me taking over this world now, remember dad. You brought me here to be Queen." Ivory snapped at her father, in a sassy kind of way and Charles seemed to caught the hidden meaning behind her words too.

His teeth crunched angry together...but then some movement caught his eye as Kaden, Trace and Tom circled Ivory. Her eyes widened at their formation.

A scroll appeared, and a bright blue light head towards Ivory-

Esmee don't know what it is but what ever it is isn't good-

Fear swept through her heart-She called out-

"CAIN HELP!" Esmee cried- and then in a huge blinding white light the scroll stopped glowing for a mere second, before it restart.

Kaden, Trace and Tom hissed trying to focus there strength on the scroll.

"Almost there. We need the key." Finding out the riddle in the scroll, the key to the kingdom is what they need, and the true heir will have the said key.

Ivory felt weak and weaker and Esmee tried to move her feet towards the scroll only to be caught up in the light and the upcoming event. The air tighten within her throat as she scream once again-

"CAIN PLEASE!" She didn't know why she's screaming his name of all names.

Then suddenly a strong hand reached her's jerking her out of the light. She gasped, finding her savor. It's Cain Heartwell and he looked at her with the worry face she have known.

"Esmee, are you alright?" He asked, only to meet the hug she tackled him in. She buried her face within his chest.

"Please save mom."

Chapter 27: His Love and Her Life

The light from the scroll that Esmee read a hour ago, slammed into Ivory and another painful scream left her lips. The light beaming off and on for some reason, causing her pain. The cause of her pain made Esmee's heart fall-she shook Cain's shirt, didn't notice that he knew a pair of wings and a weapon.

"Please Cain. Please...Please." She repeated to him, begging. He has the strength that she herself doesn't have.

Cain looked at the woman who is in more physical pain, and a wave of disgust filled his being at the sights of demons and the demon woman that is dying once again.

"Cain...Please. Help." The girl within his arms is different, he couldn't deny that, but he felt an urge to reject this and carry her away from here, but the pleading in her voice told otherwise.

That demon is her mother? He thought that her mother is dead.

His throat tighten and he shook. He didn't know what to do now. His original plan is to save and bring Esmee back with him.

He tried to decide on the right choice, but the right choice in his head is different from her's. If this is her mother than that means that Esmee is half demon.

He wanted to push her away, and make a fly or ran for it and never look back. He wanted to destroy and kill the demon race, but knowing that SHE is one of them make him be in an emotional battle he really doesn't need at this moment.

"I-I can't" The words left his mouth as the scream of Esmee mother filled the air.

Her grip loosen on him and her eyes looked up at him with fear, shock and betrayal.

The look of betrayal torn his heart.

"Why?" She whispered.

126

"I just can't." The answer seems hesitating one, and Esmee blinked back the tears. The Cain she looked up to is this awful being.

"She's my mom." was all she said, before charging to Charles, grabbing his free hand.

"Your her father! Do something!" She screeched, but all Charles did is jerked his hand from Esmee hold and gave her a hard look.

"She deserves this fate."

"No one deserves this...I do it then," Esmee declared, she closed her eyes and suddenly two huge batlike wings appeared on her back and with hyper speed she flew within the light in seconds.

Cain just stared at her back shocked. The scroll that Diamond gave him to give for her laid forgotten in his pocket.

Esmee is a demon.

Shes is one of them.

The creatures of evil.

He came here to rescue a demon...

His head begins to ache and soon Esmee's scream filled his head. His eyes snapped towards the bright circle of light.

Esmee arm stretch open with her body covering the demon woman, who looked at her with shock and fear.

Ivory placed her hand on Esmee's cheek softly-

"Please stop this dear, this is the last thing I want to happen." She whispered, but Esmee shook her head hard, crunching her teeth painful trying to cover up her screams of anguish.

"No...I...lost...you...once...I'm...not...losing...you...again." She said between huge breathes, and then suddenly a huge hand flew to Kaden's side knocking him off his feet which the circle is broken, breaking the spell. Esmee and Ivory fell to their knees both of there eyes looked dull and yet almost out of life. Cain stood over Kaden's side with a cold glare.

But it's already too late. Ivory passed out and moments later Esmee did.

Kaden bit back a laugh and so did Tom. Trace stayed quiet for some time, looking at Esmee and Ivory's bodies. Where was the key?

"Even when you grow some wings, your already too late, Heartwell." Laughed Kaden.

Cain eyes snapped to the two fallen forms on the roof top. One of them begin to move...The demon woman opened her eyes weakly, no key above her head.

"Boss! There is no key!" Trace called out surprised and Kaden's laughter died. A look of both surprise and anger appeared on both Slades faces.

"What! It can't be! She's the true heir of the demon releam!" Hissed Kaden angry to Trace.

Cain wanted to kill them all, but a sudden emotion slammed in him. Concern and Worry. Why isn't she moving?

Ivory sit up and looked down at her daughter's fallen body. Her eyes widened and she

128

tried to shook her. "Esmee, honey. Wake up."

Her skin grew pale, and the realization of what had just happened almost made Ivory roared up in anguish and destroyed everything.

Cain flew rushly towards Esmee side, surprising Ivory. He paid her no attention but instead he shook her instead.

A small gold key appeared blinking above Esmee's head.

Blinding everyone.

"That's the key to the demon realm!" Trace called, and before anyone could do anything Ivory figure tips reached the key, brushing over it when it fell to the palm of her hand. The glow stopped glowing, and then she cried. She cried openly-

"This is her life." She sobbed out to Cain.

Cain heart stopped beating emotionally. NO!

Kaden rushed up to Ivory reaching for the key only to be punched by Cain, so hard that he flew. Anger rose within Cain blood. He growl loudly, scaring everyone. Ivory placed the key on Esmee's chest, trying to push it back in but it wouldn't go back.

"You! You scum! You demon trash! You killed her! You die! I'll kill you all!" He screamed, tears came down his eyes and suddenly his sword appeared within his hands and he went on a rampage, taking Tom out first without much fight. He was the easiest of the two.

Elani, opened her eyes snapping out of the comatose state she been in only to be met with Tom fallen bloody body ontop of her's. A terrifying scream left her lips and she fainted.

Trace took out his sword in defense as Kaden took out his claws.

Cain went after Trace first and Trace dodged a few blows and barely blocked a few swings.

"Cousin, I didn't killed her. Calm down."

"You took part of it!" and with extra speed he struck Trace's chest. Deep cut appeared through the shirt and he fell backwards bigtime.

Kaden was next and he didn't put a fight much like the other two did, but he met Cain blows with his claws. On his third strike back, a huge crunch can be heard and one of his claws breaked- making him fly back in surprise.

Cain charged back in and this time it was Charles. He didn't care who he took down, someone is going to pay.

Ivory hugged Esmee tightly to her chest.

"This wasn't suppose to happen" She cried to herself.

"We have to retreat." Trace hissed to Kaden, holding his chest in pain.

"Agreed." Kaden replied and then the area surrounded with smoke, both Kaden and Trace disappeared within the smoke, using it as cover.

Charles easy dodged Cain blows with almost no effort but he didn't strike back. He flew within the smoke and he too left Cain.

"Young man." Ivory voice called out to Cain, but Cain was still too far in to be snapped out just by that sentence.

"its Esmee,"

and then he calmed himself down, emotional pain came back when he spot her lifeless body on the floor with her mother. He didn't felt any hatred for the two of them at all...He just couldn't hate Esmee.

He kneed down on the floor, dropping his bloody weapon.

He watched her painful face transform into a peaceful one. She's really is gone...

He leaned down, his lips inches from hers that his breathing reached her face. She's pale and so dull. He shivered...Remembering how much she helped him.

Just this once, he would like to repay her back for how much she did for him.

His emotions were now different.

It's changing among-sadness, anger, friendship,hurt,pain and then love.

The last emotion surprised him.

He pressed his lips against hers, his eyes closed and he let himself fell ontop of her. He kissed her very emotionally, hoping for any sign of life. He then pulled back slowly- She was still warm...It's like Jen all over again.

"You really love her." Ivory whispered sadly, she watched the scene.

Cain sit back up touching his lips and nodded his head slowly and grimmly, did love her in a way that is not the same like Jen.

131

She is special to his heart.

"I do...If there anyway I could do to bring her back to life...I do anything." Cain whispered, he couldn't believe that he didn't understand his own real feelings until now, and accepting it. He closed his eyes once more-suddenly a wave of memories came to him.

Her smile, her laughs and her voice.

Yes he would stop denying now, and just accept it even if it's too late now.

"There is away to bring her back you know...It's a old way...but it might work if a man love her so much than his own life." Ivory muttered-

and Cain ears went alert and he almost became desperate.

"Tell me."

and Ivory didn't waste anytime to tell him what he should do.

then a sudden vision of Esmee's betrayal face flashed in Cain's mind and he have to make this up to her...someway.

He was very sorry.

"To save her life, you have to take your own life with the keys to demon realm." She slipped the gold key to Cain's hand and that was all he need to know.

He looked down at Esmee's lifeless body,and kissed her lips once more liking the feeling that send in him. He wished she was alive..This was his fault anyway...If he listened to her and save Ivory when she asked him to, she wouldn't be dead.

"I'll do it."

Epilogue

The light in the room blinding her when she opened her eyes. She blinked a few times before sitting up in the bed she was in. The memories of what happened last time came flying back to her and she searched her room. Where is she? The walls of the room is plain white and the curtains were opened.

She's was at the hospital.

Confusion was all she felt now, as she touched her forehead feeling the fabric of the bandage. She then feel her back and felt no such wings.

She closed her eyes tightly trying, to pop open her wings but couldn't. The door of the hospital room opened after the second knock. A nurse, the same one that came and treat her like last time did.

She smiled at Esmee widely holding a vase of flowers-lilies in her hands.

"How did you sleep?" She asked, friendly and Esmee shook her head.

"Alright..." She answered, watching as the nurse place the flowers on the bedside table.

"Someone brought you these, today," The nurse handed Esmee a white card and she opened it up, feeling like this had already happened before.

The card was blanked, and then another knock was on the door.

Esmee looked at the nurse surprised- "Miss. What happened to me?" She asked

133

unsure, and the nurse frowned. "You can't remember? Your step mother thrown a plate at your forehead last night." She frowned.

Esmee blinked back the upcoming tears, at a sudden thought struck her. She didn't dream of all that fighting and mission her her head.

The door opened, the nurse left and her once best friend Aly walked in with a rose.

"Your fine?" She asked, worry laced her tone. Esmee nodded her head, as she placed the rose in the lilies.

"Thank you...Aly...Have you see Mr. Heartwell?"

"Mr. who?"

Esmee eyes met hers sharply-

"Our History teacher last year."

Aly shook her head- "Esmee, the name of our history teacher last year is Mr. Williams."

and then Esmee felt her body dropped back and her eyes watered.

She knew Mr. Heartwell is real. She didn't dream him up at all. He just have to be real.

Her heart twisted-She felt her heart breaking each second now. What happened after she passed out or whatever? What did God do?

'He took him away from you.' the shock of that thought almost send Esmee back in a comatose state of mind again.

A sob left Esmee's lips unwillingly-

"Esmee what's wrong?" Aly cried, hugging Esmee.

"It hurts!" She cried out, not talking about the cut on her forehead, but the emotional pain she's feeling now.

He's gone.

Gone from her life.

~.~

Hours Before...

The moment Cain touched the key to his heart is the moment his life had ended. He saw his life flashed through his eyes and when his body dropped to the castle rooftop and saw her eyes opened sleepy and then went back now to a slumber.

He was now at the Gates. He blinked, looking around. His heart went heavy, and the huge gates above opened.

"Enter for your judgement Cain Heartwell."

and so he did. He's dead. He knew for sure, seeing he's walking inside of heaven's gate by it, it seems to await for judgement.

When he walked inside, a room met him. In the middle was a huge brown desk with a small chair in front of it.

Another being is on the otherside of the chair, most likely 'God'.

"Take a seat please." and so he did. Cain felt nervous, and other than that scared for many other things.

"Cain Heartwell, you did both wonderful things and some bad things in your life. Your a respectful Supernatural Official...Why did you do suicide?"

That was it, he's going to hell.

He killed himself, but after that last thought he didn't care. He saved the girl he care for and that's all that matters to him.

"She was dying. I have no choice but to do so, sir. If you don't believe a word I said, watch from those portals or ask one of those all mighty angels." Cain replied.

A few intensive moments passed and Cain stayed strong.

A smile brought out of 'god' face-

"I see. I do not need to watch it happened again. I already did. You did the noble and great thing Cain Heartwell, going against your grudge and saving the one you love, while doing the right thing and for that I will grant you your wish. This Esmee person will live a normal life and so will you...You two didn't meet yet through."

This was enough for Cain to jumped out of his seat in happiness.

"I'll be watching the good things you will do in the future, Cain Heartwell."

His body begins to fade away in a small particles of white dusk. He's returning back to his life..This time a normal one at most.

His first mission is to find Esmee once again and hopefully, she will remember him. He didn't know how these things works supernaturally.

The End

Zeitfracht Medien GmbH
Ferdinand-Jühlke-Straße 7
99095 Erfurt, Deutschland
produktsicherheit@kolibri360.de

Druck:
CPI Druckdienstleistungen GmbH
im Auftrag der
Zeitfracht Medien GmbH
Ein Unternehmen der Zeitfracht - Gruppe
Ferdinand-Jühlke-Str. 7
99095 Erfurt